"Don't even think about saying you're not pretty enough." The pads of his thumbs stroked her cheeks, lulling her into a submissive trance.

The night before, she had dreamed about kissing Nash, their lips mating.

"You are one of the most desirable women I have ever laid eyes on," he said, his head tilted and his mouth hovering over hers. "So wh[illegible] you otherwise lied."

Nash's mout[illegible]asy surged throu[illegible], as if he had all t[illegible]essed hers with a p[illegible]ing what he wanted. Her b[illegible] into his, and she found she no longer wanted to pull away. His tongue tasted like wine and peppermint as it explored the inner recesses of her mouth, soft, thick lips pleasing her way beyond her dream.

Books by Sharon C. Cooper

Harlequin Kimani Romance

Legal Seduction

SHARON C. COOPER

spent ten years as a sheet metal worker. And while enjoying that unique line of work, she obtained her B.A. in business management with an emphasis in communication. Sharon is a romance-a-holic and loves anything that involves romance with a happily-ever-after, whether in books, movies or real life. She writes contemporary romance, as well as romantic suspense, and enjoys rainy days, carpet picnics and peanut butter and jelly sandwiches. When Sharon is not writing or working, she's hanging out with her amazing husband, doing volunteer work or reading a good book (a romance, of course). To read more about Sharon and her novels, visit www.sharoncooper.net.

SHARON C. COOPER

HARLEQUIN® KIMANI™ ROMANCE

To the other two-thirds of "Charlie's Angels"—authors Candace Shaw and Delaney Diamond—So glad we're on this ride together! Love you ladies!

ISBN-13: 978-0-373-86359-4

LEGAL SEDUCTION

For questions and comments about the quality of this book please contact us at CustomerService@Harlequin.com.

Printed in U.S.A.

Dear Reader,

It's not often you meet someone who will welcome a stranger into their home, especially a troubled teen. Iris Sinclair in *Legal Seduction* is just that type of person.

When I created Iris's character, a stunning woman who has never considered herself beautiful thanks to an event during her childhood, I knew she had to be paired with a hero like Nash Dupree, a sexy hunk who oozes self-confidence. The chemistry between the two can only be described as hot and combustible! Nash is used to getting what he wants, and though Iris might have a soft spot for anyone in need, she's no pushover. Nash soon realizes he has his work cut out for him!

I hope you enjoy reading Iris and Nash's story as much as I enjoyed writing it.

Stop by www.sharoncooper.net and find out what I'm working on these days.

Enjoy!

Sharon C. Cooper

Hugs and kisses go out to my best friend,
who happens to be my awesome husband!
Al, my dear, thank you for your unwavering love and
your immense tolerance during my writing journey.
I love you more than words could ever express!

To Yolanda Barber: Thank you for your continued support,
encouragement, and ALWAYS being willing to light a fire under
me whenever I think about dragging my feet!

To my SUPER supportive family: I love you all.
Thanks for always being in my corner!

Chapter 1

"Has the jury reached a verdict?"

"Yes, Your Honor, we have."

Defense attorney Iris Sinclair stood slowly and motioned for her seventeen-year-old client to do the same. She had logged more hours in this murder case than she had in her last few cases put together, and was confident that they would win.

Still seated, her client Terrance Gibson tugged on the collar of his light blue button-down dress shirt and yanked on the striped tie, loosening it from around his neck. He took a deep breath, grabbed hold of the edge of the table and pulled himself up, knocking a file folder to the floor and sending Iris's pen flying across the tabletop in the process.

Horrified, he glanced at Iris, his troubled eyes wide. He made a move to retrieve the folder, his chair scraping loudly against the hardwood floor before she halted him with a reassuring pat on the back. “Leave it,” she mouthed silently and smiled.

He managed a small smile back and after a deep breath, turned his attention to the jury foreman.

“We the jury, find the defendant, Terrance Gibson, not guilty of the charge of first-degree murder.”

Cheers went up around the courtroom and Terrance dropped down in his seat, his face in his hands and his shoulders shaking as he sobbed. Iris’s heart went out to him while she swiped at her own tears. It had been one of her toughest cases, but she proved, without a shadow of a doubt, that her client was not guilty. She was relieved that it was finally over and an innocent young man wouldn’t spend the rest of his life behind bars. Terrance’s only mistake the fateful night that he was arrested for murder was that he had succumbed to peer pressure and attended a house party instead of going home after a football game.

Terrance threw his arms around Iris’s neck. “Thank you for everything. I don’t know what I would’ve done without your help.”

Iris hugged him back. “It was my pleasure.” She pulled back. “Just make sure I don’t see you back here again.”

“You won’t,” he said before he went to go join his family.

Iris gathered her belongings, preparing to leave the courthouse. Despite her best efforts, she always tried not to get emotionally involved in her cases, but it was usually inevitable. One of few defense attorneys in the Atlanta area whose defendants were mostly teenagers and good kids who ended up in bad situations, Iris’s clients often got caught up in the wrong crowd, or made one bad decision, as in Terrance's case.

"Attorney Sinclair, we'll never be able to thank you for all you did for Terrance through this horrible ordeal," Mr. Gibson said to Iris when he pulled her off to the side. "We knew our son was innocent, but for you, someone who didn't know him the way we know him, to take on his case based on Terrance's word alone, means more to me and his mother than we could ever express."

Iris smiled. She had connected with Terrance and his family from day one, promising to do whatever she could to prove his innocence.

"It was my pleasure, Mr. Gibson. Terrance is a good kid. When I saw and heard the pain behind every word that he said while describing that night, I sensed he was telling the truth." If proof of innocence wasn't available, Iris relied on her gut to decide whether or not to take on a case.

She stuck around for a few more minutes before leaving the courthouse.

Back at the offices of Thomas, Alston & Sinclair, Iris moved down the wide hallway, her heels sinking into plush carpeting as some of the associates congratulated her on her victory. Though appreciative of all of the laudatory comments, she couldn't get to her office fast enough. A slight headache had been her companion for the past hour, and exhaustion after working long nights had finally caught up to her.

As she approached her office area, she couldn't help but reminisce about her professional life over the past few years. It had taken nine years of hard work at the firm, and the last four as a partner, to not only make it to the top floor of the office building, but to also receive one of the prime corner offices. Amazing views of North Buckhead and the Perimeter made the accomplishment even sweeter.

She stopped at the desk of her assistant extraordinaire, Melissa Rand. Melissa smiled and held the telephone receiver between her shoulder and ear while she gathered a padded envelope and a small package from her desk. She handed Iris the items and a small stack of phone messages as she fielded questions from a caller.

"Congratulations. I'll be in your office shortly," Melissa mouthed silently to Iris and then jumped right back into her telephone conversation without missing a beat.

Iris nodded and walked the few steps to her office. She placed her briefcase on the floor next to her long mahogany desk and quickly scanned her phone messages. Seeing nothing urgent, she tossed them on the desk before dropping into her seat. This would be the first day in over eight months that she'd leave the office before five in the evening and she could barely contain her excitement. Court dates always wore her out and this case had taken an emotional toll on her. Now that Terrance's trial was over, she could officially start making plans for her long-overdue vacation.

Her cell phone rang from inside her briefcase and she pulled it out of the side pocket.

"Hello."

"Hey, sis."

A smile lifted the corners of Iris's lips at the sound of her younger sister's voice. Janna Morgan was a supermodel who had become internationally known after her appearance in a *Sports Illustrated* swimsuit issue.

"Hey, yourself. Where are you?" Janna planned to spend her three-week vacation in Atlanta, and Iris couldn't wait to see her.

"I'm still in New York, but I should be in Atlanta by seven this evening. Do you want me to have the driver bring me to your office or to your penthouse?"

Janna had been expected the day before, but a last-minute scheduling conflict with a modeling shoot forced a change of plans. Iris hadn't seen her foster sister in three months and was anxious to hang out with her and their other sibling, Macy, this evening.

Iris glanced at her watch. *Three-fifteen.* "I'm hoping to leave here in the next hour and plan to head straight home. Why don't you meet me there and then we'll drive out to Alpharetta and meet up with Macy?"

Janna sighed. "Are you sure you're going to be there, Ms. Workaholic? The last time I ended up at your place, you didn't show up until two o'clock in the morning, and I was left in that big ol' apartment by myself with nothing but microwave popcorn and a diet soda. Maybe I should just head out to Macy's crib and you get there when you can."

"No," Iris blurted out. She wanted Janna to stay with her and knew that if she went to Macy's, their sister would talk Janna into staying with her for the duration of Janna's visit. "I promise, I will be there…but make sure you have your key, just in case."

Iris couldn't imagine her life without her sisters. She had been shuffled from one foster home to another after her single mother was killed by a misguided teen and none of their family members had been willing to take her in. Finally, Iris ended up with Mama Adel, her foster mother, who had provided Iris with a loving home and more attention than she had ever received in her life before. Iris was fourteen at the time and had joined two other girls at the house. Janna was then five and Macy was fifteen.

"Why do I need my key if you're going to be there?" Janna asked.

Iris laughed. "I promise I'll be there, but since you're staying a few days, it's best you have your key so that you can come and go with no problems." They talked for a few more minutes before disconnecting.

Noelle Beckett, one of the partners at Thomas, Alston & Sinclair and one of Iris's dearest friends, breezed through Iris's open office door. Stylish, intelligent and full of life, Noelle was a fireball, always ready to take on any challenge. She had an insurmountable amount of energy and the tenacity of a pit bull. She would zone in on what she wanted and wouldn't give up until it was hers.

"I'm glad you're smiling and sitting down."

The smile dropped from Iris's face. "Why?" She shook her head and threw up her hands in mock surrender. "No, don't tell me. I'm sure I don't want to know. Just keep it to yourself until I leave." Iris stood and began stuffing files into her briefcase. Tired, hungry and long overdue for time off from work, she had no intentions of taking on any more cases until after her three-week vacation. She slung her bag over her shoulder and then grabbed her purse to leave. Noelle blocked her path.

"Too late." Noelle flipped long blond hair over her shoulders, handed Iris a file and sat in a guest chair facing the desk. "I know you're planning to knock off early today, but we have a situation." Noelle tugged her short skirt toward her knees, defeating her purpose when she crossed one tanned leg over the other.

Iris groaned and dropped her bags near her desk before reclaiming her seat. "We always have a situation," she mumbled and opened the thin file. She lifted a magazine from it and held it up. "What's this for?"

A wicked smile curved Noelle's ruby-red lips. "Do you know who that is on the cover?"

Iris frowned and laid the magazine on top of the open file folder, and stared into the face of one of the most famous—and beautiful—men in the country. "Nash Dupree. So?"

"*Sooo,* that delicious eye candy wants to hire you to take care of a legal matter."

"Nash Dupree? *The* Nash Dupree?" Iris's clients included numerous high-profile people in the Atlanta area, but none who could match the wealth or the good looks of Nash Dupree.

Noelle grinned. "Yes, the tall, dark and sexy business mogul and president of Dupree Enterprises, who has graced the covers of almost every national magazine there is, contacted us a short while ago." Noelle twirled the pen between her fingers and swung her leg back and forth. "He wants *you*."

Iris lifted a perfectly arched eyebrow. "Excuse me?"

Noelle laughed. "He wants you to handle his niece's case. Although—" her friend placed both feet on the floor and leaned forward in her seat, putting her elbows on the desk "—once he lays eyes on you, he will probably want more than legal counsel."

"Oh, please." Iris waved her friend off and scanned the information sheet that one of the assistants had most likely put together. Mr. Dupree's fifteen-year-old niece, of whom he was the legal guardian, was arrested for drug possession.

"Don't 'oh, please' me. I hate when you do that!" Noelle banged her fist against the desk. "You are one of the smartest, most accomplished and selfless women I know, and don't get me started on how gorgeous you are! If you would give the men out here half a chance, they would be knocking each other over to get to you."

If it wasn't Noelle, it was one of her sisters saying the same thing. Iris in no way saw herself as gorgeous, but to let one of them tell it, she was every man's fantasy. Sure, she wanted to find her Mr. Right, fall in love and live happily ever after, but she lived in the real world. There was no way a man as *hot* as Nash Dupree would give her a second look. She was too tall and not skinny enough, and her skin was too dark. From what she'd seen, he only dated rod-thin, light-skinned women who made her look like the ugly stepsister, which was how she felt most days. Growing up with two "cute" foster sisters had done nothing to help Iris's low self-esteem.

She glanced back at the magazine cover. Nope, no one who looked half as good as Nash Dupree had ever asked her out. She set the magazine aside and folded her hands on top of the file folder.

"Let's get back to Mr. Dupree," Iris said. "I mentioned to you and Kyle a couple of weeks ago that I wasn't taking on any more cases until after I return from vacation. And just glancing at this information about the Dupree kid, either of you or one of the associates could handle this with your eyes closed."

"When I talked with Mr. Dupree, I offered my services, but he insists you're the one he wants. Have you ever met him?"

Iris shook her head as she glanced back at the information in the file. "Never. Did someone refer him or did he say exactly why he wanted me?"

"I don't know if anyone referred him. I just assumed he wanted the best." Noelle smirked, but shrugged when Iris narrowed her gaze. "Face it, Iris, you are the best. You not only have heart, but you're the only defense attorney who can connect with these teens."

Iris cocked her head. "What is this, Stroke Iris's Ego Day?"

Noelle stood and tugged on her tiny skirt. "It should be. You have been winning cases left and right. With the victory today, the phones will be ringing off the hook with parents who have teens in trouble, or nonprofit youth organizations vying for your volunteer services. Mercy Youth Community Center won't be the only agency begging for your time and expertise." She stopped at the door and turned to Iris. "Oh, and Mr. Tall, Dark and Handsome will be here shortly. You might want to check your hair and freshen up your makeup."

Yeah, whatever.

Iris glanced at her watch. It was going on four o'clock. Even if she were able to take on the case, by the time she heard Mr. Dupree out, it would be too late to go before a judge, which meant his niece might have to spend the night in juvenile detention. It also meant Iris might be late meeting with her sisters for dinner, and she would never hear the end of how she always put work before them.

"Iris," her assistant said from the doorway before

walking farther into the office. "Mr. Dupree is waiting for you in conference room B. Also, I talked with Mahone Construction this afternoon and put the information you requested inside your to-be-read file on your computer."

"Melissa, you're the best," Iris said to the short, thin woman whom she couldn't imagine her life without. Melissa had been with her for the past three years and she was Iris's right arm, keeping her professional life organized and her personal life drama-free. She was the person who helped maintain what little sanity Iris had left. "If I'm not out of this meeting by five o'clock—"

"I'll come a-knocking." Melissa smiled and strolled out of the office.

Iris gathered the file, a notepad and her favorite pen. She would hear Mr. Dupree out, but let him know that she would have to assign someone else to his case. She moved to the door, but stopped. It wasn't every day she had the opportunity to meet someone like the sexy Nash Dupree. She doubled back to her desk and whipped out the mirrored compact from her purse, checked her makeup and freshened her lipstick. She might as well look her best when she broke the news to him.

Iris walked into the conference room, intending to greet Nash Dupree and promptly refer him to another attorney, but a deep, baritone voice halted her the moment she stepped across the threshold. She quickly glanced around the room, thinking that Barry White himself had to be there, but he wasn't. Instead, standing on the other side of the room, talking on a cell phone, was a man whose voice made her toes curl. The deep, melodious tone was strong and intoxicating. She had always been a sucker for a man with a mysterious, sexy voice.

So this is Nash Dupree. Though his body was slightly angled toward the window, she couldn't help but notice how his broad shoulders tapered down to a narrow waist and how his long legs seemed to go on forever. Tall for a woman, Iris didn't often come in contact with men she had to look up to, literally. With one hand holding his cell phone and the other stuffed casually into his pants pocket, he appeared confident and relaxed, despite his family's recent legal issues.

"Alright, I guess it has to be this evening. Just let me know where," Nash said to the caller. He turned away from the window, but was looking down and hadn't noticed her.

Iris took in his honey-brown complexion, black wavy hair cropped close to his head, and his perfect body. The magazine photos and the few times that she'd seen him on TV hadn't done him justice. He looked every bit the powerful man that the media portrayed him to be. As for the playboy reputation he had garnered in the tabloids, she could see why women threw themselves at him. He oozed virility and wealth.

Ogling him from across the room felt unprofessional, but she couldn't help herself. Spending most of her days in her office or in a courtroom hadn't allowed her much opportunity to socialize, especially with someone who looked like Nash Dupree.

"Oh, wait, can you also let..." Nash started, but stopped when he looked up and spotted Iris. For a moment, all he did was hold the phone and stare at her. His gaze slowly traveled over her from the top of her head down to her three-inch navy blue pumps and then back up to her eyes. A small smile lifted the left corner of his tempting mouth and Iris's pulse quickened at the effect that his smile had on her. "Uh, Nigel, let me call you back."

Nash disconnected the call and placed his cell phone in an inside pocket of his suit jacket without breaking eye contact. The optimism Iris had in her ability to assign Nash Dupree to another attorney was slowly slipping away. Her breath caught as he moved smoothly across the plush room with the swagger of a self-assured, influential man who was used to getting what he wanted.

Good Lord, this brother is fine.

"Hello, sorry about that," he said in that rich voice and extended his hand. "I'm Nash Dupree."

Iris self-consciously ran her sweaty palm down her skirt and cleared her throat before shaking his hand. "Iris Sinclair. It's a pleasure to meet you."

"The pleasure is all mine."

Okay, just stay cool, Iris told herself. She smiled and eased her hand out of his grip before stepping over to the conference table and setting her notepad down. Despite her professional success, she had never been very comfortable around good-looking men, especially men who openly checked her out, the way Nash was doing now. Men like him rarely looked at her the way he was doing.

"Please have a seat." She gestured for him to sit in the high-back leather chair to her left. "I understand your niece has gotten herself into a little trouble."

"Yes, you could say that." Nash unbuttoned his suit jacket and waited until she was seated at the head of the table before taking his seat. He reached into his wallet and pulled out a photo, sliding it across the table to Iris. "That's my niece, Tania Dupree. She's an amazing young woman who is highly intelligent with musical skills that could rival Alicia Keys, and she has the stubbornness of a mule. She's the love of my life, and the bane of my existence."

Iris smiled. In the picture, Tania wore her hair in micro-braids that easily flowed past her shoulders. Hazel eyes, similar to Nash's, shined with a youthful glint, and Iris would bet her paycheck that the sweet smile gracing Tania's lips got her whatever she wanted from her uncle.

Iris handed the photo back to Nash. "She's beautiful." *Like her uncle,* she wanted to say, but kept the thought to herself.

"Thank you," Nash said quietly, staring at the photo.

"I can tell she means a lot to you." Iris crossed her leg and turned her body toward him. "Why don't you tell me what happened?" The least she could do was hear him out before assigning someone else to the case.

"Mr. Dupree?"

Nash's head snapped up and he looked at her as if he had forgotten she was in the room. He stood and rubbed his hand over his head and down the back of his neck.

"I'm sorry. I, um, it's been a helluva day." He chuckled and Iris nodded her understanding, realizing for the first time since leaving court that the headache she'd been battling for the past couple of days had finally departed. "Anyway, I received a call a couple of hours ago that Tania had been arrested for drug possession. She and some of her classmates had a half day of school and were heading home when they were pulled over by a cop."

"Why were they pulled over?"

"From what I understand, the kid driving the vehicle didn't come to a complete stop at a stop sign." Nash shoved his hand into his pants pocket, taking Iris's attention from his sexy hazel eyes down to the front of his pants. She quickly diverted her attention. *What the heck is wrong with me?*

"The cop probably would've just issued a warning," Nash continued, "but when one of the kids started smarting off, the officer made all them get out of the car."

Nash roamed around the plush space. "I told Tania to stop hanging out with those kids. Associating with them had already gotten her into trouble at school. A few months ago, she was apprehended by the cops when one of the little thugs she was hanging out with stole a couple of candy bars from a convenience store."

Nash stopped and slowly turned to Iris, releasing a loud sigh. "When Tania exited the car, she swung her backpack onto her shoulder and a bag of marijuana fell to the ground. Supposedly it came from her bag. Needless to say, all the kids claim they knew nothing about it and they all were taken into custody."

"What did Tania say when you asked about the drugs?"

Nash walked back over to the table, but didn't reclaim his seat. "She said it wasn't hers and had no idea how it made its way into her bag."

Iris asked a few more questions, taking notes as he talked more about how he had transferred her to the best private school in Johns Creek, a suburb outside Atlanta. Tania had had her share of harmless trouble since arriving at the school, like putting a dead bird in one of her teachers' desks and getting caught egging another student's car.

"I can't believe she's been arrested for drug possession with the intent to sell. She's too smart for that and has never shown any sign of drug use. I know that weed wasn't hers."

"So you believe her?"

"Without a doubt, but don't get me wrong, I understand that the cops had to take her in. Having drugs in her possession doesn't look good. The worst part is, the officers would have let her leave with me, but she was adamant about staying until she talked with a lawyer." He let out a harsh laugh that lacked humor. "That girl became indignant with an officer because she didn't like the way he automatically accused her. As if he didn't have reason to doubt her damn story!"

He pounded the table with his fist and turned away. "I'm sorry," he said when he turned back around. "This whole situation is like a bad dream."

"I'm sure it is." Iris could tell how much this was bothering him. "I assume they're keeping her in detention until she goes before the judge." That was more of a statement than a question. Georgia's juvenile detention system didn't care who your parents were. They didn't tolerate unruly behavior. If a child was uncooperative, that often meant an automatic night in detention.

Nash nodded and folded his arms across his chest. "You have to understand, Attorney Sinclair—Tania is very headstrong, but she's a good kid."

"I don't doubt that, Mr. Dupree." Iris glanced at her notes and sighed. It would only take a few minutes to meet with Tania and then go before the judge and get an arraignment date set, but Iris had vowed not to take on another case until after her vacation. If she took this case, then there would be another, and yet another one after that. She would end up spending another year without taking any much-needed time off. She placed her pen on top of the notepad and leaned back in her seat, folding her hands on top of the table.

"Mr. Dupree, based on what you've told me, any one of our associates will be able to assist you and your niece. Not only will it save you money, it will—"

"I don't give a damn about the money, Counselor!" Nash leaned on the table. His face was a glowering mask of anger, hovering only inches from hers. "I want my niece to have the best representation there is. Refusing to take the case is not an option."

Iris bristled at his tone, the arrogance behind his words making her see red. She stood slowly, trying to contain the anger that suddenly bubbled within her. She pinned him with a level look, willing herself to remain calm. "With all due respect, Mr. Dupree, I'm not sure what you're accustomed to, but I decide what cases I take on and I will not stand for you or anyone else telling me what I can or cannot do."

Nash stood so close to her that she could smell his mint-scented breath against her face. His expression was unreadable, and his enticing lips were close enough to kiss. He glanced down at her mouth before he lifted his eyes to meet hers.

"But I want you."

Chapter 2

Nash could feel the fuming heat emitting from Iris's body. He didn't mean to raise his voice, but after an exhausting day his patience had snapped. Looking down into the most intriguing brown eyes that he'd ever seen, he wanted nothing more than to reach out, pull the enchanting attorney into his arms and taste her tempting lips.

When she first walked into the room, he thought there was no way this Nubian goddess could be the defense attorney his niece had insisted on him hiring. He had been surprised when Tania gave him Iris Sinclair's information, stating that she was the best. Despite the seriousness of Tania's drug-possession charges, he couldn't help but fantasize about all that he could do with the tall, curvy bombshell standing before him.

The old saying "the darker the berry, the sweeter

the juice" had immediately come to mind. Her smooth, dark skin made him want to touch her face to see if it was as soft as it appeared.

Staring into exotic eyes that held so much fire…all that did was stoke the flames she had ignited within him when she first walked into the conference room. He couldn't help but admire the way she was standing her ground, not even flinching at his tone despite the anger he could see brewing in her eyes. Iris glanced away and ran her fingers through her shoulder-length curly hair, pushing an unruly strand from her face before taking a drawn-out breath.

"Mr. Dupree, I'm flattered that you have chosen me to represent your niece, but right now I'm not taking on any new cases. Based on what you've told me, Tania sounds like a good kid. Since this is her first offense, all she'll probably get is a hefty fine and a short probation, and she might have to endure a couple of court-ordered drug classes." Iris gathered her notepad and pen. "She doesn't need me. We have associates who are more than qualified to handle this type of case."

"If I wanted just any lawyer to handle my niece's case, I would've found someone else, but apparently you don't understand, Attorney Sinclair. I don't want just anyone. I want *you*."

"We don't always get what we want now, do we, Mr. Dupree?" she asked flatly. The look she gave him said she wasn't afraid of him and didn't give a damn about what he wanted.

Not accustomed to hearing the word *no,* Nash turned away and chuckled. He hadn't become a successful entrepreneur by accepting no for an answer. If anything, the word made him work harder to get what he wanted.

Looking back at Iris, who was still glaring at him, her chin held high, her resolve unwavering, he could only imagine the type of respect she demanded, and received, in the courtroom. He definitely had to have her as his niece's attorney. They were two of a kind, Iris and Tania. Both clearly had a stubborn streak, and neither was afraid to stand up to him.

Nash ran a hand down his chin. Apologizing wasn't something that came easy for him, but if he wanted to get this stunning lawyer to reconsider, he'd better make nice and do some serious groveling. Besides, he already liked her—maybe a little too much.

"Please forgive me, Counselor," he said and moved back to the table where she was still standing. "I was way out of line and I meant no disrespect. Just give me a chance to explain why having you on this case is so important." He gestured to the chair she had vacated. After a brief hesitation, Iris reclaimed her seat. "When I went to pick up my niece from juvie, she refused to leave. She said that she wasn't leaving until she spoke to a lawyer, and not just any lawyer, but you. She's the one who gave me your information."

Iris shook her head and as low smile tilted her lips. She glanced away before looking back at him. "Mr. Dupree, without even meeting Tania, she reminds me of myself at that age—fearless, determined and at times unyielding."

"Yeah, I sensed that a few minutes ago when you looked like you wanted to strangle me. I recognized the look. I've been on the receiving end of it many of times from my niece."

Iris sat back in her seat and chuckled. "I have to admit, I am a little curious about this niece of yours."

"I know you don't have to take on Tania's case, and I respect your need to be selective in the ones that you do accept, but I hope you'll reconsider."

"I'll tell you what." She gathered her belongings and stood. "I'll meet Tania at the detention center in the morning and hear her story. Then we can decide next steps."

Nash buttoned his suit jacket. "That's all I ask."

Iris tugged on the tight-fitting, low-cut dress. Janna had brought it and insisted that Iris wear it tonight. Being out on a Thursday night was unusual, but she couldn't pass up the opportunity to have dinner with two of her favorite people.

She glanced around the dimly lit restaurant. Servers moved about efficiently, taking customer orders, refilling water glasses and clearing the tables, each adorned with a centerpiece of a single candle. Lately, her professional life had taken over her world. A typical evening consisted of staying late at work or spending the evening at home with Chinese food and a glass of wine while reviewing case notes.

"I can't believe you were able to pull her away from work and get her here on time," Iris heard Macy say. "This has to be a first."

Iris rolled her eyes. "Would you two quit? It's not like we never get together for dinner."

"Okay, so when was the last time we got together for dinner, all three of us?" Macy asked, looking over the top of her designer eyeglasses. A strand of long brown hair with auburn highlights fell into her face before she quickly pushed it behind her ear. Macy and Janna were on one side of the tall-backed leather booth, while Iris sat across from them.

"You finally decided to get those reading glasses. They look good."

Macy pushed them up farther on her nose. "I know you're trying to change the subject, but thank you. I finally broke down and bought some. Those medical charts were getting blurrier by the day. Now, getting back to my original question—"

"It's not my fault we haven't gotten together. Ms. World Traveler over here—" Iris nodded her head toward Janna "—is the one who hasn't visited her big sisters in months."

"Okay, don't start on me. Aren't we supposed to be celebrating?" Janna chimed in and lifted her glass. She had naturally long, wavy hair, smooth cinnamon-brown skin and big, bright eyes shaded by long eyelashes. "I want to propose a toast. To a kick-ass defense attorney who continues to prove that she's the best there is."

"Here, here," Macy said, and they clinked their glasses together.

Janna's comment caused Iris to reflect back on her conversation with Nash Dupree, who labeled her as being the best. She wondered if he had noticed her staring at him throughout the conversation earlier today. Sure, she had been listening, but there were times she had tuned out and had zoned in on his magnificent lips…and that smile. He had the most beautiful, straight teeth she had ever seen on a man, which only enhanced his crooked, cocky grin. And those intense hazel eyes that missed nothing. Add those features to his alluring deep voice, and he was irresistible. God, what she would give to go home to a man with that voice who could talk dirty to her while....

"Hel-lo," Macy said in a singsong voice, waving her hand in front of Iris's face. "Are you still with us?"

Iris blinked several times and reached for her glass of water. Instead of bringing it to her mouth, she wanted to lay the cold cylinder against her cheek to cool the warmth that had spread to her face.

"You were smiling pretty hard there for a minute, sis," Janna said. "So, what, or who, were you thinking about? Inquiring minds want to know."

Iris had never fantasized about possible clients—or their guardians—before. She'd better get a grip. Talk about unprofessional. "Nobody," she finally said.

"Mmm-hmm. That was a heck of smile for it to be about nobody. You know you can tell us," Macy goaded. "Besides, it's about time you met someone who makes you smile like that."

Iris gave Macy a "drop it" look, but then noticed the way Janna was smiling. "And you're talking about *me being happy!* What's with you grinning from ear to ear like you have a secret that you're dying to share?"

"Oh, I spotted an old friend who just walked in," she said, patting her hair before she whispered, "Quick, do I have anything in my teeth? He's coming over." She flashed a smile at Iris.

"You're good."

Before Iris had a chance to glance back to see whom her sister was primping for, Janna slid from the booth and stood.

"Well, hey, there, stranger," Janna greeted a tall gentleman, whose broad shoulders and long arms swallowed her up in an embrace. His back was to Iris, but his intoxicating, woodsy scent smelled mildly familiar.

Janna stepped out of his hug, but kept her hand on one of his arms. "It's been a long time."

"Yes, it has." The stranger's deep, melodious voice was familiar and captured Iris's full attention. "I'm surprised to see you in Atlanta. Are you doing a shoot here?" he asked Janna.

"No." Janna grabbed his other arm, turning him toward the table. "Actually, I'm here visiting my sisters. Let me introduce you."

Iris's heart slammed against her rib cage when the pair of hooded hazel eyes she'd been daydreaming about zoned in on her. *Nash Dupree.* Of all the restaurants in Atlanta, how is it that they ended up at the same one?

"This is my sister, Dr. Macy Carter, and my other sister, attorney Iris Sinclair."

"Nice to meet you," Nash said to Macy, shaking her hand before turning to Iris. "It's good to see you again, Counselor." He grasped her hand and Iris shivered when he brought it to his lips, kissing the back of it as he gazed into her eyes.

Iris stared back at him, enraptured by his attention and forgetting that they had an audience. When Macy cleared her throat, Iris quickly pulled her hand from Nash's and dropped it into her lap. "It's nice seeing you again, Mr. Dupree," she sputtered, feeling, more so than seeing, her sisters' gazes on her.

"Nash. Please call me Nash."

"You two know each other?" Janna asked.

"Actually, we met this afternoon," Nash volunteered, but before he could elaborate, the maître d' of the restaurant informed him that his party had arrived. "I'm sorry. Though I would love to spend more time with you three lovely ladies, duty calls." He kissed Janna on the cheek, bidding her a good evening, and then his gaze met Iris's. "I look forward to seeing you again soon," he said before he moved away from the table.

Iris watched him strut away with a swagger that had not only her mesmerized. Every other woman he passed—whether they were with a date or not—turned and eyed him from head to toe.

She turned back to her sisters, not surprised that they were staring at her. A hint of a smile lifted the edge of Janna's mouth.

"Well, well, well, Macy, I think someone has been holding out on us. What do you think?"

"I think you're right and if Ms. I-Don't-Have-Time-for-a-Man doesn't start talking soon, I'm going to have to give her one of my famous back-in-the-day beat-downs."

Heat rose to Iris's face. She quickly lowered her head and cut into her T-bone steak, shoving a chunk into her mouth. "So, how's your pasta?" she asked Macy.

"Don't you dare try changing the subject." Janna leaned across the table and whispered, "How do you know Nash?"

Iris sighed, knowing her sisters weren't going to let the subject drop until they had some details. Though she hadn't officially agreed to take on Tania's case, she was seriously thinking about it. That, at least, gave her the excuse that she couldn't give much detail. "He came to see me about a legal matter."

"Well, it looks like he's interested in changing it to

a personal matter." Macy grinned and lifted her wineglass to her lips.

"That's not going to happen."

"Why not?" Janna asked. "He's suave, he's the sweetest man I know, he's wealthy and apparently he's interested in you. What's the problem?"

Iris narrowed her eyes at Janna. "Even if I were interested, which I'm not, I wouldn't consider hooking up with him, knowing that you two have a history."

Janna frowned. "I've never dated Nash. We've done a few magazine ads, a voice-over gig together, and he was my escort for one of Victoria's Secret Angels events, but outside of that—" she shrugged "—nothing. We've never kissed, unless you count a kiss on the cheek."

Iris scrutinized her sister. Though she believed her, she couldn't imagine Nash Dupree not being attracted to Janna. She was a supermodel, for God's sake. Men had always clamored for her attention, even when they were kids. Because of their nine-year age difference, Iris could remember how different her little sister's high-school social life had been from hers. Then, Iris couldn't pay a popular guy to give her the time of day, whereas Janna had actually complained about all the attention she received.

"Iris, he's not the playboy the media make him out to be. Sure, he's been seen with various women—"

"Not just any women," Iris interrupted, "but famous, ridiculously gorgeous women."

"That doesn't mean anything. The same as it doesn't mean anything when the paparazzi snap pictures of me and my dates or escorts. Ninety-nine percent of the time, it's business, and I'm sure that's the case with Nash. He could have dated a few, but it likely wasn't serious. He has to be in the public's eye to promote his nightclubs and all of his other business ventures, including his new clothing line. Iris, he's nothing like how the media paint him."

"How do you know?" Iris asked. If Janna hadn't ever gone out with him, how could she be sure he wasn't a playboy who tossed women aside like old newspapers?

"I know. Though we never dated, when we worked together, conversation came easy for us. So I know him. We're friends. Now, don't get me wrong, he loves women, but he's not the type to lead women on or to be seriously involved with more than one at a time."

"Face it. You have no excuse not to go out with him," Macy chimed in.

"He hasn't asked me out," Iris said, more to herself than her sisters. If Nash's playboy reputation, despite Janna's reassurances, wasn't enough to make Iris steer clear of him, the fact that she might represent his niece was all the more reason to slow her roll and this line of thinking.

Nash Dupree was as popular as a rock star, and he captured female attention wherever he went. Why was she even entertaining these thoughts? She shook her head. *What is wrong with me? He would never be interested in someone like me.*

Nash Dupree glanced across the semicrowded restaurant at Iris. He had a clear view of the table where she and her sisters were dining. He and Nigel Montgomery, chief operating officer of Dupree Enterprises and Nash's best friend, were at a trendy restaurant in Midtown Atlanta to hear an internationally known jazz group perform. Nigel had insisted on his hearing them before the group left to go on a two-month European tour promoting its latest CD. The COO wanted the group to play at the grand opening of Platinum Pieces–Buckhead, Nash's fourth jazz club, which was scheduled to open in four months. This location would also include a fine-dining restaurant. It was his second club in Atlanta, adding to a total of four; the other two were located in L.A.

Nash stole another glimpse at Iris while Nigel took a phone call. She must have felt his gaze on her because she glanced over at him. He grinned and a shy smile graced her lovely lips before she quickly looked away. What were the chances he'd get to see her twice in one day? And if he thought she was *fine* back at her office, tonight she was absolutely stunning. He could tell by the number of men who had stopped at the sisters' table that apparently he wasn't the only one who had taken notice. Granted, some of them had stopped to talk with Janna, but Iris, wearing a low-cut dress showing off her long, graceful neck and tempting breasts, was receiving her share of attention. She didn't come across as a woman who would be caught in a tight-fitting garment, but he'd be damned if she didn't have the perfect assets to fill it.

"She's a beauty," Nigel said, following Nash's line of vision when Iris stood and walked across the restaurant toward the restrooms. "Do you know her? You've been staring at her for the past ten minutes. Why don't you do what you usually do and go over and ask her out?"

"I would if she wasn't possibly going to be Tania's lawyer."

Nigel's eyes grew large. "*That's* the defense attorney? Hold up. That tall, curvy, celestial being is the one who might be representing Tania?" Nash chuckled at his friend's facial expression. "Hell, she doesn't look like any attorney I've ever seen."

"How you gon' be ogling a woman as married as you are?" Nash tasted the martini that he hadn't touched. "What would Dawn say?"

Nigel and Dawn were the poster couple for happily ever after. Married for ten years, the two were always stealing kisses, holding hands or sharing naughty looks. At times it was almost nauseating to witness their public displays of affection, but on the other hand, it was nice to see two people so very much in love.

Nigel took a swig of his beer. "I might be married, but I'm not dead. There's no harm in looking. Besides, the woman is kind of hard to miss. Actually they all are," he said, referring to Iris and her sisters. "And isn't that Janna Morgan, the supermodel, at their table?"

"Yep, they're all sisters. The other one is a doctor." Nash looked over again just as Iris returned to the table. He still couldn't get over how good she looked in the skintight red dress. She definitely didn't look like a defense attorney tonight.

Nash turned his attention back to Nigel. "So when is this group going to perform? Today has been a crazy long day and this mess with Tania has made it even longer."

"Well, I hate to break it to you, but I think your day is about to get worse. Don't look now, but your ex, the not-so-lovely Eve Vanlough, just walked in."

Nash glanced over his shoulder and groaned. If he didn't know any better, he would think she was following him. They broke up over two months ago and lately Eve surfaced at the most inopportune times, claiming her sudden appearances were a coincidence. He didn't believe in coincidences. It was time to nip this nonsense in the bud once and for all.

Eve stopped at their table. "Well, funny meeting you—"

"Cut the crap," Nash growled and stood. He gently grabbed her by the elbow, pulled her out of the main dining room and didn't stop until they were in the atrium. "I don't know what the hell you're up to, but I suggest you back off. If I go to one more place and you show up, I'm getting a restraining order."

"Oh, Nash, sweetie, aren't you being overly dramatic?" she said in that whiny tone that always grated on his nerves. She moved in closer, straightening his tie before running her hands down his chest. "I can't help that we like the same restaurants. I'm here meeting a friend and I just happened to see you and your shadow in there." She nodded toward the table where Nash had left Nigel. "I figured the least I could do is go over and say hello. Besides, I've missed you."

He grabbed hold of both of her hands and backed her into the corner, away from the entrance. "Eve, when are you going to stop playing these games? This is one of many reasons why we're not together. You don't know when to back off."

Her heavily made-up face screwed up in anger and she jerked out of his grasp. "If you break up with me, you're going to be sorry!"

"Excuse me?" He narrowed his eyes at her. "I'm the last person you want to threaten, and for the record, we broke up months ago. Apparently you haven't grasped that fact yet."

She glared at him as if her little five-foot-six self

could intimidate him. That lasted a whole five seconds before she changed her tune.

"I'm sorry." She pulled a tissue out of her purse and dabbed at her invisible tears. "This breakup has been really hard on me. I thought we had something special, that we would one day get married."

Nash relaxed his shoulders and sighed. She had to know her tears no longer affected him, but maybe if he tried a different approach she'd finally get the message.

"Listen, Eve, I didn't mean to hurt you, but you knew going in that I wasn't interested in anything serious. I was up-front with you from the beginning. I'm not looking to get married to you or anyone else."

Thanks to his college sweetheart, Nash had promised himself years ago that he would never allow a woman full access to his heart again. He and Audrey had dated their first year at UCLA, and talked about getting married upon graduation. During their last year of college, Audrey dumped him for the school's star quarterback, whose family came from old money. She told Nash she wanted to marry rich, instead of marrying someone who had the potential of being rich.

He would never forget how she took his love and his heart and stomped the hell out of them. The only thing good that came out of the experience was that it spurred him to work his butt off to become a successful multimillionaire.

"Nash, honey, I know you said you weren't interested in marriage, but I thought..."

He placed his hand against Eve's cheek, suddenly feeling sorry for her. She leaned into his touch, shutting her eyes and then reopening them as she met his gaze.

"I'm sorry, Eve. I hate things turned out the way

they did, but I can't do this anymore." He dropped his arm and turned to walk back into the restaurant, but flinched when a camera flash blinded him.

"Mr. Dupree…Mr. Dupree…Mr. Playboy Dupree. Is this your latest victim who you're kicking to the curb?"

Damn. Nash ducked his head, put his arm up to block any additional photos and hurried back into the restaurant. This was the second time in the past couple of weeks that he'd been bombarded by some paparazzo mentioning him being a playboy. Now that he thought about it, Eve had been there then, too.

Hours later, Nash sat in the office at Platinum Pieces–Midtown, his first Atlanta nightclub. To get his mind off women, he was catching up on paperwork. He sifted through documents and reviewed report after report from his business managers, hoping to make a dent in the pile.

"Okay, boss, all the patrons are out and everything is locked up," the club's manager said from the doorway. "We're going to head out. You coming?"

Nash glanced at his watch, noting the late hour, and then glanced at the short stack of file folders on his desk. "Nah, I have about an hour of work left. You guys go ahead and I'll catch up with you tomorrow."

His manager hesitated. Tall and burly, he looked more like a wrestler than a club manager. "I can stick around for another hour. Just holler when you're ready to leave."

Since one of the female servers had been mugged late one night when leaving the club, Nash had instituted a policy: no one, regardless of gender or age, left the building alone after closing time. While spending most of his days and evenings at the new location, he'd temporarily forgotten the rule. Nash wasn't too concerned about his safety. The club, located in Midtown Atlanta, had good exterior lighting. Growing up in Compton, California, he had learned at an early age how to take care of himself, but he didn't want to be the one to start breaking rules.

"Actually, give me fifteen minutes to wrap things up."

Nash should have been done with his paperwork hours ago, but his mind kept drifting to Tania—and Iris. This couldn't have been a worse time for Tania to get into trouble, not that there ever was a good time. Nash was swamped with getting the new club and restaurant open, and the last thing he needed was to be worrying about her at juvenile detention. And then there was her lawyer. *Iris*. Even her name was sexy. How was a man to concentrate when visions of her took up so much space in his mind?

Always a sucker for a beautiful woman, he couldn't help but wonder about the alluring defense attorney. Meeting her earlier at her office and then seeing her again at the restaurant was like experiencing two different women. One minute he was dealing with a reserved attorney and the next, a voluptuous babe.

That's how Nash envisioned the lovely Iris Sinclair—a stuffy professional by day, fighting for her young clients, and a sex goddess at night, taming her man with her lasso of truth before wearing his ass out. *Oh, yeah.* Nash grinned at the thought. He leaned back in his seat, swiveling his chair back and forth, enjoying the mental visual until his cell phone rang.

Unknown caller. He started to let the call go to voice

mail, but thought better of it, in light of Tania's being in detention.

"Hello." He adjusted the single-lightbulb desk lamp away from his face.

"Hi, Nash."

Nash dropped his shoulders and let his head fall back against the leather headrest of the office chair. *Why me?*

"Eve, why are you calling? Especially this time of night?" What was it going to take to get her to move on?

"I couldn't sleep and knew you were probably up working. I was thinking that maybe you could stop by and put me to sleep like you used to."

"Eve, the days of me stopping by your place, for any reason, are over. You have to figure out a way to move on. I have."

"How can you say that, Nash? We dated for eight months and now you're saying it meant nothing to you."

"I'm not saying that at all. Eve, you knew going in that I didn't want anything serious." Nash felt like a broken record. They'd had the same conversation for the past few weeks and he didn't know what else to say to make her understand.

"I know what you said, but we had something special. You can't tell me that the sex wasn't good."

Nash would admit it had been good at first. She was an attractive, sexy woman who had a wild, adventurous side. It was everything else about her that he couldn't deal with. Her jealousy and accusing him of seeing other women was a huge turn-off. Until she came along, he hadn't dated exclusively since Audrey. Two months into dating her and he remembered why.

She constantly complained about him not spending enough time with her and she showed up at his place of business demanding his attention. That was enough to drive a sane man crazy. The last straw had been when she talked about them getting married and alluded to sending Tania to a boarding school. *Now that's never going to happen.*

"Eve, you and I are over. Besides, if I remember correctly, we only were dating for four months, and eighty percent of that time was me dealing with your childish behavior and your insecurities."

"I can change," she said, her high-pitched whine grating on his nerves.

Even if she *could,* he wasn't interested. He wasn't looking for anything serious with any woman, especially someone like Eve.

"You might be able to change, but I've moved on, and I suggest you do the same."

A beat passed before she spoke. "If you think you can use me until *you've* had enough and then kick me to the curb, you have another think coming. We're not over until I say we're over," she screamed.

Nash cursed under his breath. "Eve." When she didn't respond, he called out to her again before he realized she had hung up. *Damn. Please don't tell me I have a psycho on my hands.*

Chapter 3

The next morning, Tania Dupree sauntered into the small meeting room at the detention center. She wore a long-sleeved T-shirt and a pair of worn, fitted jeans, looking as if this was just another ordinary day. She hugged her uncle and then moved around him to get to Iris.

"Hi, Attorney Sinclair. It's a pleasure to meet you, and thank you for coming."

Iris shook her hand, pleased with Tania's manners and assuredness. This young lady oozed poise and self-confidence, so unlike Iris when she was that age. Tall and thin, Tania, like most teenagers, suffered from a mild case of acne over her caramel complexion. She had an easygoing demeanor, but her hazel eyes assessed everything and took it in.

"I didn't think you would come," Tania said, "but I

knew that if anyone could convince you, it would be my uncle." She glanced at Nash, giving him a crooked grin.

Iris didn't bother telling her that, though her uncle's persistence played a small part, it was mainly Iris's curiosity about Tania, and just maybe, her desire to see Nash again that was the deciding factor.

Iris gestured for her to have a seat on the opposite side of the table. "Tania, why don't you explain to me why you were willing to spend the night in detention when you didn't have to, and why you insisted on seeing me."

"I'd like to hire you."

Iris was a little taken aback by her take-charge attitude, and stole a glance at Nash, who didn't appear surprised at all.

"Someone is trying to frame me. I have never done drugs and have no interest in starting now. *And* I definitely had no intent of selling or delivering marijuana like the officer accused. I know the State of Georgia has a low tolerance for people who have anything to do with drugs, and the penalties for possession of more than an ounce is a felony and can get you one to ten years. The amount of weed on me was less than an ounce, but it wasn't mine and I need your help in proving it."

Iris sat back, stunned but impressed. She glanced at Nash, who just shook his head and shrugged.

"That's why I need you as my lawyer. I saw you on the talk show *Atlanta Right Now* a few months ago. You had a cool, dark gray pinstriped suit on, with a pair of fly gray shoes that had a strap around the ankle. I was like..." She stopped and shook her head. "Anyway, you mentioned that most of your clients are my age and I got the feeling that you really cared about them."

"You're right." Iris smiled, amused by the young woman's recap of her attire and pleased with her insight. "I care very much about my clients and do everything I can to prove their innocence."

"Cool," Tania said and grinned.

Iris pulled a file out of her briefcase and laid it on the table. "Since I'll be representing you…" She let the rest of her statement hang out there for a moment, and didn't miss the pleased look on Nash's face. "Let's talk about what you can expect when we go before the judge. Based on what you and your uncle told me, I assume you're pleading not guilty."

Tania nodded.

"Though you had a run-in with the law a few months ago, and caused all types of drama here yesterday—" Iris raised an eyebrow at Tania "—I think the judge will go easy on you."

"Why won't this go to trial? I want to prove that someone planted those drugs on me."

Iris studied her for a moment. "Tania, do you know where the drugs came from? Do you know who might have planted them on you?"

Tania hesitated. "No, but I want to find out. I plan to start my own investigation into the matter once I'm out of here."

"Hold up," Nash said in that deep voice that made Iris want him to never stop talking. "I don't know what's going on in that head of yours, but don't think about doing something crazy. I don't want you confronting anyone, or worse, accusing someone. You're in enough trouble as it is, and I'm not planning on going through this nonsense again. If you end up in jail, I'm going to insist they keep you."

Iris explained the best- and worst-case scenarios to prepare Tania and Nash before they faced the judge. "The police officer you gave a hard time to yesterday referred the case to juvenile court. When we go in for the arraignment hearing, you'll enter a plea agreement and the judge will probably place you on probation, recommend some type of counseling or have you perform community service. I will inform the judge that this is your first offense and request that the charges be dropped. Since they found less than an ounce of marijuana on you, this is considered a misdemeanor. Hopefully you'll receive no more than probation and possibly a small fine."

"I know twenty percent of the cases referred are usually dismissed or handled informally. What if this case has to go through formal proceedings? Will you still represent me if it goes to trial?"

Again, Iris just stared at her young client. "Are they teaching law in high school these days?"

A shy smile reached Tania's lips. "Nah, I read a lot about women in law and I plan to be a defense attorney like you someday."

Iris's heart melted. "Wow, I don't know what to say."

"If you keep getting into trouble, you can forget it," Nash said to Tania. "How are you going to get into law school if you're sitting in a jail cell somewhere?"

Tania tilted her head. "Uncle Nash, I said I was sorry. This won't happen again, so you don't have to keep using the jail threat."

An officer opened the door and stuck his head in.

"Attorney Sinclair, the judge is ready to meet with you and your client."

"Thank you," Iris said and gathered her notes, placing them in her briefcase. She looked at Tania. "Are you ready?"

"Yes, ma'am."

"After you." Iris directed Tania to the door.

"Do you see what I have to go through?" Nash mumbled close to Iris's ear, causing goose bumps to skitter down her back. She wondered what it would be like to wake up to that deep, hypnotic voice every morning. Her steps faltered when she tried to shake her wayward thoughts free.

"You okay?" Nash asked, placing his hand on her elbow to help steady her.

"Yes, I'm fine." She discreetly moved her arm out of his grasp and walked beside Tania. Nash followed close behind. She couldn't wait for this hearing to be over so that she could get away from the likes of Nash Dupree, and the lustful thoughts that plagued her mind whenever he was around.

Nash watched Iris in action. She looked stylish yet professional in a black pinstriped skirt suit with a white button-down blouse opened at the neck and pearls. From his vantage point, a bench right behind her and Tania, the skirt accentuated her shapely derriere, making it almost impossible for him to pay attention. After ending his relationship with Eve a few months ago, he had vowed to stay clear of women and focus on his businesses, but Iris made that hard to do. She intrigued him and he wanted to get to know the sexy vixen who hid behind business suits and seemed to have a shy side about her.

"Excuse me, Your Honor?" he heard Iris say, her voice suddenly strained. Nash sat up straighter, wondering what he had missed.

"I said I think it's in the best interest of this child if she's removed from her uncle's home until after the review hearing," the judge said.

"Now, wait a minute!" Nash sprang from his seat. "There is no way in hell I'm letting you or anyone else take her from me."

"Have a seat, Mr. Dupree, before I have you removed from these proceedings," the judge said in the same monotone voice.

"No! I can't have a seat when you're talking about taking my—"

"You've been warned, Mr. Dupree. Please have a seat."

Panic rioted within Nash like a volcano on the verge of erupting. There was no way he could sit back and let them take Tania from him. She was his everything. He yanked on his designer tie, loosening it while the room seemed to close in around him and his breath solidified in his throat. What in the hell had happened? This arraignment hearing was supposed to be just a formality.

When Tania was born, his twin brother and his sister-in-law chose him to be Tania's godfather, asking him to be her caretaker if anything should ever happen to them. He would never forget the way his heart swelled when he'd first laid eyes on her. The miracle of life overwhelmed him and he knew at that moment there was nothing he wouldn't do for that little girl. But when he'd agreed to be her godfather, he had no idea six years later her parents would be killed during a tsunami in Japan.

It'd been nine years and his chest still tightened whenever he thought about his brother. Not only had he lost his twin, who was also his best friend, but he had to try and explain to a little six-year-old why her parents were never coming back. Now this judge was threatening to take the one constant in his life and the only family he had left away from him? They might as well lock him up now because there was no way he'd sit by and watch them take her, especially not without a fight.

"Your Honor," Iris chimed in. "With all due respect, I don't think it's a good idea to remove my client from her home. She's a good kid and I have gotten to know both her and her uncle and I can see that Mr. Dupree loves this young lady more than anything. He's given her a good home and the best edu—"

"I don't doubt Mr. Dupree loves her, Counselor, but I don't see where he's giving her the type of attention she apparently needs," the judge explained, as if Nash weren't sitting there. The more Nash heard, the angrier he became. "It's clear that Tania is an intelligent young lady, but the trouble she's been getting into lately tells me that something is missing in her life, and I think that something is attention and order."

The three of them listened as the judge gave Tania a stern lecture about her past social behavior, as well as his concern about this last incident and the direction she was heading. When he was done with Tania, he started in on Nash. He commented on the type of lifestyle Nash lived and how he paraded around with numerous women.

"Over the next three months, I want both Mr. Dupree and this young lady to go through counseling—first individually, and then as a family. We'll schedule the first review hearing for six weeks. Once I get reports back from the therapist, as well as the assigned probationary officer, I'll decide if further disciplinary actions are needed."

"Your Honor." Iris took a long breath before continuing. "Where are you proposing Tania stay during this time?"

"She can stay with a dependable relative, or we can contact Family Services."

"No!" Iris, Nash and Tania said in unison.

"I'm sorry, Your Honor," Iris spoke up, and wrapped her arm around Tania's shoulder when Tania started to cry. "As a person who has personally lived in one foster home after another, I don't think placing Tania in a foster home is in her best interest. Mr. Dupree is all the family she has and they are good together."

"Well, what would you suggest we do with her, Attorney Sinclair?"

Iris bit her bottom lip and glanced at Tania, then back at Nash before returning her attention to the judge. "She can stay with me."

A tense silence filled the small room. *Shock* wasn't a strong enough word to express what Nash felt at Iris's proposed solution. He had seen how quickly she and his niece bonded before going into court, but he couldn't believe what she was volunteering to do. There was no way he could object because at the moment he had no other ideas. Even if he had, one more outburst might very well land him in jail.

"This is an unusual request, Counselor." The judge ran his hands over his thinning gray hair, then removed his eyeglasses. He gnawed on the temple tip in deep thought, looking from Iris to Tania and stealing a glance at Nash. "But…I'll allow it. Actually, I think you might be good for this young lady."

What was I thinking, agreeing to become Tania's temporary guardian? Iris thought after the judge dismissed the court, placing her cell phone back into her briefcase. No, she knew exactly what she was thinking. She didn't want to see Tania go from foster home to foster home the way she had after her mother was killed. At fourteen, Iris had been angry at the world. Though academically smart, she wanted nothing to do with school and had skipped a large chunk of her freshman year of high school. Thank God she had finally ended up with Mama Adel, her last foster mother and the one woman who made a difference in Iris's life.

Iris released a shaky breath and planned her next move. She made a quick call to her office and talked with Noelle. The judge had agreed that it was probably best that another attorney from Iris's firm oversee Tania's case going forward and, after hearing what happened, Noelle gladly agreed to take over.

Iris glanced at Nash and Tania, huddled together at the end of the courthouse hall. She didn't have a clue how to care for a child, especially a fifteen-year-old girl, who, according to her uncle, was a borderline genius. All Iris knew was that she couldn't let Tania end up in foster care.

"Thank you," Nash said to Iris when she approached him and Tania. Nash had his arms around Tania and Iris couldn't tell who was comforting whom. This couldn't be easy for either of them. According to Nash, he had had custody of Tania since she was six years old and he was all she had.

A strong desire to be wrapped within Nash's arms herself came over Iris and it took all she had to maintain some distance. What the heck was wrong with her? Each time she looked at him, her stomach did somersaults and she couldn't understand—why him? She was about to take on one of the biggest challenges she had ever faced, and here she was fantasizing about being in his strong arms. It didn't help that she was seeing a softer, more compassionate side of him that she hadn't seen the day before.

"Tania, sweetheart, have a seat over there." Nash pointed toward a bench ten feet away. "I want to talk with Attorney Sinclair for a moment," he said, kissing the top of Tania's head before releasing her.

"Thanks for doing this," Tania said and wrapped her skinny arms around Iris's waist.

Iris hugged her back, getting emotional at the gratitude she felt with Tania's simple gesture. "It's my pleasure."

When Tania stepped away, Nash moved closer and Iris inhaled the fresh Irish Spring soap scent that clung to him, making her want to move closer to get a better whiff. *God, he smells good.*

"You shocked me in there," he said quietly and released a ragged breath.

Taller than most women and the average guy, Iris wasn't used to being near a man who towered over her, but she loved how feminine it made her feel. She looked up and into Nash's eyes. She saw something in him that was much different from the man she'd met yesterday, who had been confident, in control and, at one point, downright arrogant. Now, with haggard eyes, he looked like a man who had weathered a serious storm and who couldn't seem to find the words to express what he was feeling.

"I don't know how I'll ever be able to thank you," he said. "Had they taken my baby and put her in foster ca..." He rubbed his forehead, emotion flitting across his face before he cleared his throat and continued. "I probably would be in jail right now. You have no idea what you did for us in there and I don't know how I'll ever be able to repay you."

"I'm glad I could help." Iris fidgeted under the heart-rending tenderness in his eyes. She still couldn't believe she had agreed to be Tania's guardian, but right now, seeing how grateful Nash was, she was glad she had volunteered. "The next few months are going to be interesting. I don't have a clue as to how to take care of a teenager, especially one who is as sharp as Tania."

Nash chuckled and it was the first time in the past couple of hours that she'd seen some semblance of the powerful man from the day before. "Well, according to the judge, I'm not the person to ask." A moment later, he turned serious. "I have to tell you, I wanted to strangle that guy. He clearly has bought into all that crap the media have everyone believing. The judge didn't know a damn thing about me and as far as I'm concerned, he based his decisions today on misinformation. I'm not the self-centered, skirt-chasing playboy the media make me out to be. That guy has no clue about the number of nights I have sat up with Tania when she was sick, or how I never missed a piano recital, a parent–teacher conference or her basketball games."

Iris didn't miss the bitterness behind his words and

wondered just how far off the paparazzi in their rendering of Mr. Nash Dupree were. Listening to him now, he did not sound like the same man the tabloids depicted. He was describing a different person. She took it all in, but knew that time would tell and the real Nash Dupree would be revealed.

"What happens now?" he asked.

"Well, since the judge approved having one of the partners at my firm oversee Tania's case, Noelle Beckett, who is also a good friend, will be working with us. We'll take care of the necessary paperwork this afternoon."

Iris leaned her back against the wall and held her briefcase in front of her, resting against her thighs. If only she had known the judge would threaten to take Tania away, she would have prepared some type of defense. In a juvenile-arraignment hearing, the arbitrator had the authority to take the liberties that Judge Sanderson took. Iris glanced down at her black leather pumps and then up at Nash.

"I'm sorry about what happened in there. Judge Sanderson is usually very fair. Considering the offense, I had no idea the hearing would go in that direction and I'm so sorry I didn't better prepare you and Tania."

Nash stood in front of her, his muscular body blocking her view of people walking up and down the hall. "Attorney Sinclair—"

"Iris," she said. "Since we're going to be coparenting over the next couple of months, we should probably be on a first-name basis."

He flashed that irresistible grin that made her pulse thump harder. "Iris…I hope you're not blaming yourself for what happened in there, because I don't blame you. If anything, without your quick thinking and willingness to step in and help us, the hearing would have gone a helluva lot differently."

Iris knew he was right, but still she didn't like to be blindsided, and Judge Sanderson had totally caught her off guard. Now she and Nash had to make the best of the situation. Iris glanced up at Nash to find him studying her. She diverted her gaze and pushed away from the wall, hoping he would take a step back, but he didn't. Instead of saying "excuse me," she sidestepped him, but ended up grabbing hold of his arm when she tripped over his foot.

All muscle and all man. His hand covered hers, which was still holding on to his arm. Electric jolts shot through her body.

"Sorry." She snatched her hand away. It had been over a year since she'd been with a man. What was she going to do with the butterflies that bounced around in her gut each time he looked at her with those intense hazel eyes? No man had the right to look so sexy. How was she going to handle the fact that she wanted to wrap her arms around his neck, rub her horny body against his and taste his enticing lips?

"So, how do you want to do this?"

Iris jerked her head up and stepped back. "What?"

He laughed and put his hands out in front of him in mock surrender.

"Can you relax? Please? You're wound tighter than a sixty-year-old spinster on her first date."

There was that smile again. Iris relaxed her shoulders. She was in a hell of a lot of trouble if he had the power to disarm her with just a smile. That settled it. She needed to stay clear of Nash Dupree now more than ever in order to maintain some type of professionalism…and sanity.

"Do you want to come by our house and get some of Tania's things, or do you want me to drop her stuff off? Either way is fine with me, although I must warn you, she'll probably want to pack herself. She pitches a fit when I even act like I'm going to step across the threshold of her precious sanctuary."

"Oh, uh, well," Iris stuttered, "I thought that maybe we'd go to the office first to speak with Noelle, and then maybe we'll head to your place." *Lord help me.*

Chapter 4

Iris pulled into a long cobblestone driveway a few hours later, awed by the most spectacular two-story brick home that looked like something out of *House Beautiful*. She had been in the Johns Creek area only a few times, but hadn't been in this part of exclusive multimillion-dollar homes.

"You can park over there," Tania said, pointing at the last of the four garage doors. Iris couldn't understand why one person needed a four-car garage. As if reading her mind, Tania added, "Uncle Nash parks his *precious* Aston Martin Vanquish in this one and he rarely drives it. It was a birthday gift to himself last year."

"Wow, that's some birthday gift."

Iris thought she had splurged on her $1,500 Louis Vuitton bag a few months ago, but that was nothing compared to spending almost $300,000 for a car.

"Hey, ladies, come on in." Nash opened the front door before Tania had a chance to use her house key. "Did Tania give you directions or did you have to fend for yourself because she was so engrossed in that phone of hers?"

If Iris thought the infamous Nash Dupree looked tempting in a tailored suit, Nash in a short-sleeved polo shirt that stretched across his chiseled chest and hugged his rock-hard biceps was downright delicious. When did he have time to work out? From what she heard, he worked sixteen-hour days as she did, yet his body looked as though it had been masterfully sculpted, while she was barely able to maintain her size-eight figure. There was no doubt he participated in some type of physical activity. His long legs, encased in jeans that hung low on his hips and accentuated his thighs, were almost too much.

"Iris?"

"Huh?" Her eyes met his gaze and she realized he probably caught her gawking at his body. She couldn't remember the last time she'd been so fascinated by a man. "Oh, I'm sorry. My…my mind was somewhere else. What were you saying?"

His mouth curved into a knowing smile. "I asked if Tania was able to get you here without being on her cell phone the whole ride."

A smile found its way through Iris's embarrassment when she remembered how much she enjoyed Tania's company during the ride. "She steered me in the right direction and I'm happy to say she didn't get on her phone once. We talked all the way here."

"Now that I find hard to believe."

Nash closed the door behind them and Iris glanced

around the impressive foyer. She took in the spectacular teardrop crystal chandelier and elegant twenty-foot columns that stood on each side of the entrance into the main part of the house. The imposing dual-curved staircases evoked the splendor of the room and drew her eyes up to the tall beamed ceiling.

"Uncle Nash, you act like all I do is talk on the phone." Tania's voice brought Iris back to the present. "Where's Gram?"

"In the kitchen." Tania kissed her uncle on the cheek, dropped her backpack near the staircase on the right and took off around a corner.

On the ride there, Tania had told Iris about their housekeeper, Ms. Dalton, and how she was more like a grandmother than anything else. When Tania's parents died, Ms. Dalton stepped in to help Nash with Tania. Since Nash's parents had died some years earlier, Ms. Dalton, a good friend of Nash's mother since grade school, had made herself Tania's honorary grandmother.

"Your home is magnificent."

"Thank you."

"Did it come with the beamed ceilings or did you have the beams added?"

"Added." They stood between the curved staircases, gazing up at the ceiling. "We vacationed in Spain the year after we moved to Atlanta and the vacation house we stayed in had magnificent wood beams throughout the place. I vowed then that the next house I built or purchased would have them. Come on, let me show you around."

They roamed through one side of the first floor, Nash pointing out artifacts and artwork that he acquired during his travels, giving informative details about each. When they walked past a guest room—which was in addition to Ms. Dalton's living quarters and the four bedrooms that he mentioned were upstairs—Iris wondered why three people needed so much space.

"How tall are you?" Nash asked.

Iris frowned. She wondered what brought on the unexpected question. They had just walked into his office.

"Five…nine. Why do you ask?"

He shrugged. "Just wondering." He perched on the edge of his desk and studied her as she stood in the middle of his large, masculine office, trying not to fidget under his thorough perusal. "Did you ever consider going into modeling?"

Iris laughed and turned away. "Yeah, right, like anyone would choose someone like me to model any of their fashions." The floor-to-ceiling wall of books drew her attention and she walked over to them, fingering one of the vintage tomes that occupied a shelf of other antique volumes. "The only thing I would have going for me in that industry is my height."

With two long strides, Nash was standing before her. "What do you mean, 'someone like you'?" he asked, his eyes narrowed and his hand on her elbow turning her to face him.

Iris wondered if he was serious. "Nash, you of all people know the modeling industry seeks women who are not only tall, but who are reed-thin, who have a…" She threw up her hands. "Oh, I don't know, a sexy walk and a drop-dead gorgeous face. I might be tall, but I have way too much meat on my bones. My hair is not straight enough, and I'm not pret—"

"Don't." He cupped her face between his hands, his lips only inches from hers. "Don't say it."

"Don't say what?" she asked hoarsely, her throat suddenly dry. His nearness made her senses spin and she willed herself not to lean forward and connect her lips with his. All it would take is a small tilt of her head for their mouths to meet. She knew she should step out of his grasp, but her feet wouldn't move. Heck, she could barely breathe. The intense heat from his gentle yet powerful touch against her face had her immobile. It was no wonder women flocked to him. Everything about the man exuded sex appeal and his touch, so tender, yet strong, sent a spark to every nerve ending within her body.

"Don't even think about saying you're not pretty enough." The pad of his thumbs stroked her cheeks, lulling her into a submissive trance.

The night before, she had dreamed about kissing Nash, their lips mating with an intensity of two people who were madly in love.

"You are one of the most desirable women I have ever laid eyes on," he said, his head tilted and his mouth hovering over hers. "So whoever told you otherwise lied."

Then Nash's mouth covered hers and spirals of ecstasy surged through her body. He kissed her slowly, as if he had all the time in the world. His lips caressed hers with a polished mastery, boldly taking what he wanted. Her body melted into his and she found she no longer wanted to pull away. His tongue tasted like wine and peppermint as it explored the inner recesses of her mouth, his soft, thick lips pleasing her way beyond her dream.

He moved his hands from her face, one going to the back of her head, the other to her waist, pulling her close. The logical part of her brain screamed, *Step away, Iris,* but the passionate, deprived woman in her, who hadn't been kissed this thoroughly in over a year, said, *Go for it.* Iris ran her hands slowly up his chest, loving the way his muscles rippled beneath her touch. She wrapped her arms around his neck and leaned into him, intensifying their connection.

Her body pulsed as his mouth and hands stirred a sensuous flame within her that she'd never felt with another man. Growing up with two sisters who were constantly pursued by the opposite sex when no one ever gave her a second glance was enough to make her feel less than attractive. But within a short period of time, Nash Dupree had not only made her feel desired, but also sexy. At the moment, Iris wanted to throw caution to the wind and let him have his way with her.

"God, you taste good," he mumbled against her neck, his hands cupping her butt.

A moan rose from the back of her throat when she felt his erection against her pelvis and her eyes flew open. Breathing hard, she jumped back and covered her mouth with her hands. *What in the hell is wrong with me?* His weak-in-the-knees kiss had made her forget where she was and who he was—the city's most notorious playboy. The last thing she needed was to be pulled into his seductive web and then end up with her feelings hurt and her heart broken. *Been there, done that.*

"Have dinner with me," he blurted out and took a step forward while she took a step back.

Her mind raced. She couldn't have dinner with him. Not only was he a ladies' man, he was her client's guardian. Well, technically Tania was no longer her client since Noelle had taken over the case, but still…

"No," she said, out of breath, and moved farther away. She needed to pull herself together so that she could go in search of Tania and get the hell out of there. Being attracted to him wasn't right, but damn if it didn't feel good to be in his arms. A potent shiver of pleasure skittered across her skin as she recalled how amazing it had felt to be touched by him. She knew now more than ever that she would have to keep her distance. The unfamiliar feelings she was experiencing weren't normal—she barely knew the guy and it would behoove her to discourage him from setting his sights on her.

"Nash? Nash, where are you two?" A voice came from nearby and within seconds, a short, plump woman with a toasted-pecan complexion and a friendly smile stood just outside the office. "I had to come see the infamous defense attorney whom I have heard so much about since Tania walked in," she said, and limped into Nash's office.

Nash was slow to turn away from Iris, but eventually did. "Sorry, Ms. D. I should have stopped by the kitchen with Iris before I started showing her around."

"Yes, you should have," she scolded, her hands on her rounded hips. "No matter how hard I try teaching him and Tania good manners, sometimes it feels like I'm talking to myself," she said to Iris.

Nash towered over his affable housekeeper, and though Ms. Dalton wasn't his mother, the love and respect that glittered in his eyes toward her couldn't be missed.

"Iris, if you haven't already guessed, this is Ms.

Dalton, our more-than-a-housekeeper." Nash snaked one of his long arms around Ms. Dalton's shoulders and pulled her close, placing a kiss against her temple.

She swatted at him good-naturedly. "Don't try to be all sweet and thoughtful now." She winked at Iris. "How are you, my dear? It's nice to meet you." She hugged Iris and her warmth embraced her. That, along with the smells of vanilla and cinnamon, took Iris back to her childhood, when her foster mother would greet her with a hug at the door after school.

"Thank you for what you did for Tania and Nash today." Ms. Dalton leaned back, her hands on Iris's upper arms. "Are you hungry? Sure you are," she said before Iris had a chance to respond. "Dinner is ready. Let's go."

Nash shook his head and chuckled. "She pitches a fit if we don't eat while the food is hot," he said, answering Iris's questioning gaze while they obediently followed behind Ms. Dalton.

After dinner, Nash said goodbye to Iris and Tania and closed the front door behind them, and then leaned against it. He had had a hard time focusing throughout dinner with Iris sitting across from him. She had the most arresting eyes he'd ever seen, and remembering their kiss from earlier didn't help. He couldn't stop thinking about how good her soft lips had felt against his and how perfectly she fit in his arms. Had she not pulled away, there was no telling what would have happened in his office. He hadn't planned to kiss her, but those eyes, those tempting lips and the innocence in her gaze drew him in.

He released a weary sigh and pushed away from the door.

"Now that's the type of woman you need to be thinking about settling down with," Ms. Dalton said when he returned to the kitchen.

"Aw, Ms. D., don't start," Nash groaned. He rubbed his temples in preparation for the speech he knew was coming. It was a lecture he had heard more times than he cared to remember and the topic never changed—it was time he got married. The only thing different about this version is that she actually liked Iris, which was a first. Over the years, she hadn't liked any of the few women he had brought around, especially Eve.

"Iris is smart and cute, and I can tell she's not going to tolerate any nonsense from you." Ms. Dalton placed a second slice of sweet-potato pie on the bar in front of him and busied herself around the spacious kitchen. She wiped down the granite countertop near the sink and then moved to clear the stove. "And did you notice how well Tania responds to her? That little girl needs someone like Iris in her life. Who knows? This whole mess could be a blessing in disguise."

Nash had indeed noticed how Tania hung on to Iris's every word. During dinner, Iris told them about her involvement with Mercy Youth Community Center, an organization that helped troubled teens get on the right path. Tania asked thoughtful questions throughout the conversation, wanting to know everything about the center and Iris's role in it.

How Iris found time to do community work with various youth groups, despite her hectic work schedule, was a mystery to him. He barely had time to spend with Tania, let alone other teens. Was Ms. D. right? Had he done his niece a disservice by not surrounding her with positive female role models?

Nash stuffed a forkful of pie into his mouth. He thought about the conversation he had had with Iris right after the hearing, how she felt she had let him and Tania down by not preparing them better for what had happened. Didn't she know that her selflessness in stepping in to help them outweighed any surprises that arose during the hearing? The attorneys he had met were cutthroat and itching for a fight. That wasn't how Iris came across. She was an amazing woman whom he wouldn't mind getting to know better. The problem was, he was seriously attracted to her, but she didn't come across as a woman who would agree to an affair. She was the marrying kind…and he wasn't.

"This whole situation," Ms. Dalton said, breaking into Nash's thoughts, "is all the more reason why you need to settle down and make some changes in your life. Tania needs a more stable home."

"Tania *has* a stable home," he said and stood with his dessert plate in his hands. "I would do anything for Tania and I've done my best to give her everything she needs and could ever want."

"I know, child." She tossed the dish towel on the counter, her arms folded across her ample bosom. "I'm not saying you're a bad parent, I'm just saying Tania is getting older, and she needs a woman like Iris in her life."

"She has you, Ms. D. You've been like a mother to me and a grandmother to Tania. She doesn't need anyone else."

Ms. Dalton let out a hardy laugh. "Boy, I don't know

anything about the youth of today. I hate the latest styles, I can't tell the difference between MAC makeup and some over-the-counter face paint. I might have been able to tell her about the birds and the bees, but she's going to start dating soon and will need a woman closer to her age who can help her with the dos and the don'ts of dating."

Nash almost dropped his plate at her last statement. "I already told Tania she's not dating until she's thirty, and even then, I'm not sure I'll allow it," Nash said seriously, despite his housekeeper's sympathetic smile. "I'm not kidding, Ms. D. These young punks out here are only after one thing, and I'll be damned if they pull my child into their way of thinking." He knew how he was at that age and there was no way in hell he would let some testosterone-laden kid near Tania.

Ms. Dalton took the plate from his hands and patted Nash on the arm. "You won't be able to shield her forever, son, but what you *can* do is make sure she's well prepared when dealing with boys."

"Ms. D.! I can't believe you're encouraging me to supply Tania with condoms."

Ms. Dalton turned from the sink and frowned. "I'm talking about making sure she knows how to handle herself on a date." She shook her head and chuckled, returning her attention to the dishes in the sink. "But now that you mentioned it, maybe you should arm her with a few condoms…right after you show her how to use them."

Nash hurried out of the kitchen, his housekeeper's hearty laugh echoing after him. No way he was going to stand there and let her get a good chuckle at his expense. He shivered at the thought of having any type of conversation with Tania about condoms. But if he wasn't going to do it, someone had to. *Maybe it is time I surrounded her with some positive female influence.*

Chapter 5

Iris stopped vacuuming, but didn't turn the machine off while she slid the oversize upholstered chair out of the way. She cleaned that area before moving the chair back to its original spot. She had been dusting, moving furniture and vacuuming for the past hour, working off some nervous energy. Next stop, reorganizing the kitchen.

"What is wrong with you?" Janna stood in front of the vacuum cleaner and snatched the power cord from the wall, immediately bringing Iris's cleaning frenzy to a halt. "Do you know what time it is?

Iris glanced at the clock on the wall. "Almost seven o'clock."

"Don't get cute! It is too early to be making this much racket. I'm surprised you didn't wake Tania and the whole damn building." Janna tossed the cord to the floor and folded her arms across her chest, her pajama top rising to show off flat abs.

"You have been behaving like a Tasmanian devil for the past few days and I want to know why."

Apparently, her sister didn't intend to move and Iris didn't miss the daggers Janna shot her way. Iris sighed and pushed the vacuum cleaner to a nearby corner, and then dropped down on the sofa. Leaning forward, her elbows on her knees, she covered her face with her hands. She knew her behavior over the past few days had been childish, but she couldn't help it. She still had a hard time believing that she had actually kissed a celebrity.

"I kissed Nash," she mumbled. She remembered how his sensuous lips had melded with hers and how his tongue had meticulously explored the inner recesses of her mouth, teasing, caressing and pleasuring. She sighed at the memory.

Silence filled the room and Iris peeked from behind her hands to see if her sister was still there. Seeing her standing in the same spot, her mouth hanging open, didn't make Iris feel any better.

A slow smile graced Janna's mouth and she squealed. "Tell me everything!" She dropped down next to Iris and nudged her shoulder. "I can't believe you've been holding out! Start talking."

"I don't know why you're so excited. I feel like such an idiot."

"What? Why?"

"Because I know what type of man Nash is and I let him kiss me."

"Are you kidding me? Do you know how many women would kill to kiss that man?"

Yeah, Iris knew, and it didn't make her feel any better. He had probably kissed thousands of women the same way, making them fall for his charming ways.

"That's not the worst part."

Janna raised a perfectly arched eyebrow and leaned back. "Okay," she said, stretching the word out. "What's the worst part?"

"I enjoyed it and…and I didn't want to stop." She groaned and dropped her head to her knees.

Janna fell back against the sofa laughing, a sound from deep in her belly that had her rolling around on the sofa trying to catch her breath.

"It's not funny."

Iris clenched her mouth while she watched as Janna rolled onto her side. She slapped the sofa and held her stomach while she laughed. In spite of herself, Iris chuckled. Though she didn't think it was *that* funny, she had to admit—hearing a grown woman, a defense attorney, whine about a stupid kiss was kind of amusing.

Wiping tears from her eyes, Janna finally said, "I don't get you sometimes. You have been trippin' these past few days. Cleaning the house like a madwoman, making Tania and me afraid to ask you anything for fear of getting our heads chewed off, and it's all because you shared a hot kiss with Nash Dupree." Janna shook her head and wiped her eyes with the back of her hand.

"It's not that simple. I can't go around kissing my clients or my clients' uncles, though technically they are no longer my clients, but that's beside the point."

"Then what's the point?" Janna sat back against the

sofa and crossed her long legs. "I'm sorry, but I don't see a problem here."

"Janna, Nash is way out of my league. You know the type of women he's been seen with. Actresses, models and even that senator from Los Angeles. I can't compete with those women."

Janna frowned. "Iris, you're just as amazing as any of them. Besides, what makes you think you have to compete? Has Nash asked you out?"

The dinner invitation that Iris had quickly declined came to mind. "Yes, but I turned him down."

Janna threw up her arms and let them fall to her side. "Why would you turn him down if you're attracted to him? You're so concerned about these other women, but I would bet my modeling contract that he wasn't seriously involved with them."

"That's just it. He can go out with any woman he wants, so why me?" Iris leaped from her seat and paced in front of the sofa. "I don't want to be some pity date because he feels like he has to make me believe I'm… I'm desirable or…or pretty."

"What?"

Iris then told her sister everything about the evening at Nash's place, from the moment she pulled onto his cobblestone driveway until the moment she and Tania left. Just thinking about Nash did something to her. It was like being back in high school. All of her insecurities about not being pretty enough came flooding back.

She would never forget the night she'd gone to a house party with Macy at one of her friends' house, and Jeff Kramer, the boy Iris had a crush on, was there. Iris was a freshman and Jeff, a senior. He had no clue Iris existed; well, at least not until that night. Iris's best friend had tagged along to the party with them, which pleased Iris since she didn't know many of the other people there. At one point in the evening, various board games were pulled out and the large group of kids split up into smaller groups based on which game they wanted to play. She and her best friend joined one small group, but Iris had no idea that the game they were going to play was Secrets. They each had to tell a secret and everyone else had to guess whether it was true or not. She'd only joined the group because her friend and Jeff were in the group.

"Don't tell me you're still remembering what that idiot Jeff Kramer said to you?" Janna's voice broke into Iris's thoughts.

Iris said nothing. The night of the party, her best friend had let it slip that Iris had a crush on Jeff. To say Iris was horrified would be an understatement. Jeff was the captain of the football team, an all-around star athlete and the cutest boy in school. All the girls thought he could walk on water, including her. Iris wanted to crawl under a rock when some of the girls pointed her out to Jeff after her friend's slipup. When Jeff found out who she was, he studied her from head to toe, a disgusted look on his face. Iris burst into tears when he told the small group that he wouldn't be caught dead with the big-eyed Amazon.

Macy was livid when she found out and, true to her character, she had verbally let Jeff have it. She'd gone out with him once and proceeded to tell the group that there hadn't been a second date because making out with him was like kissing a blowfish. She went even further and told Jeff that if he didn't apologize to Iris, that little piece of data wouldn't be the only information she would share about his inadequacies.

"Iris, when are you going to forget about that jerk?" Janna put her arm around Iris's shoulders. "That was well over fifteen years ago."

Iris wiped at her eyes, not realizing tears had slipped out. It might have happened years ago, but some things were hard to forget. Jeff had publicly humiliated her in front of all of her classmates and, had it not been for Mama Adel, she might have dropped out of school. She owed her foster mother everything, but for years afterward, Iris tried to keep a low profile and not draw attention to herself. She had already been self-conscious about her appearance, but Jeff's words wiped out all of her confidence. It didn't help that a couple of years ago, she overheard a guy she was dating tell someone that he was only with her because she had money. This was something she had never told her sisters.

"Just because he called you names and told you no other boy will ever want you doesn't make it true. You are a beautiful, successful woman, and Jeff was a stupid, inexperienced *kid.* Now, Nash, whew!" Janna fanned herself. "He is a grown-ass man who knows a good thing when he sees it."

Iris tried to smile at Janna's theatrics, but her heart still ached from the horrible memories. But she had to admit, Janna was right about one thing. Nash was definitely all man…and that's what scared her.

"Thanks for letting me tag along," Nash said from across the table. Instead of sitting in the restaurant, they had chosen a booth in the center of all the action within the game room. Tania had run off with a friend she spotted from her old school, leaving him and Iris to fend for themselves.

Though he had stopped by the penthouse to drop off a few items for Tania, he also was trying to find any excuse to see Iris. A few days ago, he had asked her out, but she'd turned him down. So he was surprised when she had invited him along on one of her and Tania's outings. Little had he known they were heading to Dave & Buster's, a popular restaurant, bar and arcade that offered entertainment for children and adults. It wouldn't have been his first choice of restaurant, but if it meant getting to know Iris better and spending time with Tania, he was game. He hadn't been able to get Iris out of his mind since they shared that steamy kiss in his office.

"You're welcome. I didn't think you would accept the invite." Sitting across from him at a table, she diverted her eyes the moment the words left her mouth.

"Is that why you invited me, because you thought I'd decline?" Nash took a swig from his beer bottle, finding enjoyment in her discomfort.

Iris kept her eyes on the glass of soda in front of her, moving the ice around with her straw. Nash could honestly say he had never met a woman like her. She was such a contradiction. Confident and in charge when at her office or in the courtroom, but shy and introverted when around him.

Her gaze eventually met his. "I invited you because... because I thought you would enjoy hanging out with us. If that's not the case, you're welcome to leave. We can find our way home."

The beginning of a smile lifted the corners of Nash's

mouth. "And miss an opportunity to get to know you better? I don't think so."

He watched her as she glanced around the game room. Her thick, curly hair was held away from her face by a headband, accentuating her exotic features and making him want to run the back of his hand against her smooth skin. It was nice seeing her casually dressed in a pair of designer jeans that hugged her shapely butt and a lightweight sweater that stretched across her chest. What he would give to be her sweater, resting snugly against her perky breasts.

Nash shifted, adjusting his pants, which were suddenly uncomfortable. Served him right for allowing his mind to wander.

Tania bounded up to them. "I'm going to play a game of pool," she said. Her friend from school waited a couple of feet away.

"Where are the pool tables?" Nash asked, but then glanced at Iris. "Sorry, I guess I should've let you respond. Old habits die hard."

Iris smiled. "No problem. I would've asked the same question."

"They're on the other side of the restaurant," Tania said.

Iris twisted her mouth while thinking, looking at Nash for help. When he remained silent, she said, "Okay, but make sure you don't leave this building, and I want you to check in—" Iris glanced at her watch "—in twenty minutes."

"Will do!" Tania darted away. She grabbed her friend by the arm and pulled her along.

"So, how have things been going with Tania?"

Iris broke into a relaxed smile. "Very well. We

have gotten into a comfortable routine and have only bumped heads once or twice in the past week."

Nash raised an eyebrow. "Only once or twice? That's probably a record. Normally she turns everything into a negotiation or a debate. Everything from what time she should be up to why she should be able to dye her hair purple."

Iris laughed. "I'm a lawyer and, according to my sisters, it's pointless to argue with me. Besides, I love how spirited she is."

"Spirited? Is that what they're calling it these days?" They both shared a laugh.

The server brought their food and topped off their drinks. "Can I get you anything else?" the young woman with spiked hair and an earring in her nose asked.

Iris glanced at her and Tania's meal. "No. Everything looks good."

"Can we get a few more napkins?" Nash asked.

"Of course. I'll be right back."

"Let me go and get Tania before her food gets cold," Iris said.

Nash reached out and grabbed Iris's hand before she stood fully. "I'll go and find her, but first I'd like to talk to you about something."

Iris tilted her head and sat back down. "About what?"

"About the kiss we shared at my place. I'm wondering why you're avoiding the obvious attraction we have for each other."

Nash sensed her sudden nervousness. What was with her? He didn't know her exact age, but knew she had to be in her mid-thirties, yet she was acting as though he was the first man to show interest in her.

"I don't think it's a good idea to act on this…this attraction. Our focus should be on getting your and Tania's lives back together, nothing else."

"I disagree. I believe in pursuing what I want, and what I want is to know you better."

"Why?" she asked, her voice strained, her eyes pleading. For what, Nash had no idea, but he had every intention of finding out. "Why are you doing this? Why do you want to know me better?"

He leaned across the table, still holding her hand. "What are you afraid of?" he whispered. She tried to pull away, but he wouldn't let her. "Iris, I want to know what you're afraid of."

"I'm not afraid. It's just…it's just…"

"What? It's just what?"

"You can go out with any woman you want, why me?"

Nash released her hand and sat back in his seat. That's what this was about? He didn't know what he had expected her to say, but that wasn't it. He studied her and was surprised to see that she was serious.

"Iris, I'm extremely attracted to you." He shrugged. "And I want to know you better. It's that simple."

She considered him for the longest time before releasing a breath and dropping her shoulders. "Okay."

Nash raised an eyebrow and leaned forward. "Okay? That's it? You'll go out with me?"

"One date." She emphasized, raising her forefinger. "And then you back off."

"But—"

"I'll go out with you once. That's all I'm offering.

I decide when and where. Take it or leave it," she said with finality.

Nash laughed and leaned forward. "I guess I'll take it, but I doubt once will be enough for you."

Chapter 6

Iris stood just inside the double doors of Mercy Youth Community Center, waiting for Nash's arrival. A working date was probably not what Nash had in mind when he asked her out, but she had to give him credit for going along with the idea.

Iris volunteered twice a week at the center, helping younger children with their homework and high schoolers with college applications, and often providing free legal advice to their parents. Since it was Sunday and the center was closed, she thought it would be a good time to show Nash around and get him to help her assemble bookshelves she'd purchased for the library a couple of weeks ago.

Iris gazed out the glass doors and her pulse quickened when Nash pulled into the parking lot and exited his Tahoe truck. *Could the man get any finer?* She couldn't take her eyes off him as he strolled toward the building, his gait as confident as the man himself. Dark shades shielded his eyes and the long-sleeved T-shirt fit his upper body like a well-worn glove. She licked her bottom lip, admiring how ruggedly handsome he looked in loose-fitting jeans that did nothing to hide his well-built body. *I talked a good game about only going out with him once, but he might've been right. Once might not be enough.* Everything about him had her conjuring up lustful thoughts and over-the-top fantasies that she'd like for him to star in.

"No man should be that sexy," she mumbled.

"My thoughts exactly."

Iris swung around startled to find the center's director, Stacey Watkins, standing behind her. Besides Stacey, there were only a handful of people on-site and Iris hadn't heard the director's approach. She and Stacey tolerated each other at best. Great at raising money, Stacey was a gossiping, man-hungry busybody with the personality of a gnat.

"So who is this gorgeous specimen that you're out here drooling over?" Stacey asked and leaned closer to the glass door. "Wait a minute. Don't tell me that's… Oh, my God, it is! That's Nash Dupree!"

"Hey there," Nash said, flashing his legendary smile when he stepped into the center and saw Iris. He leaned in and kissed her on the cheek, his hand on the small of her back sending a wicked wave of desire up her spine. "Sorry I'm late."

Iris thought she would melt and puddle to the floor. The heavenly scent of his aftershave and the feel of his hand against her body stoked a gently growing fire within her. It didn't help that he greeted her as though they were longtime lovers and this was just another ordinary day. Iris couldn't remember the last date she'd gone on, but she could honestly say that she had never gone out with a man who made her want to throw caution to the wind the way Nash did.

Stacey cleared her throat. "Aren't you going to introduce us, Iris?"

"Oh, I'm sorry, of course." She swallowed hard and cleared her throat, barely able to think straight with Nash standing so close. "Nash, this is Stacey Watkins, the director of the community center. Stacey, Nash Dupree."

"It's a pleasure to meet you," she said, her tone a little too cutesy for Iris's taste.

"Same here." Nash shook her hand and brought his attention back to Iris. His appreciative gaze roamed over her, and a sexy smile lit his handsome face. "It's good to see you."

Iris couldn't help but smile back, suddenly feeling comforted by his presence. "You, too."

"Seems like a nice place you have here," he said to Stacey. He eased away from Iris and glanced around the colorful entrance, stopping near a glass display case. "How long has the center been open?"

Stacey ambled up to him and began rattling off information regarding the history of the center, touching Nash's back or his arm periodically and tossing out fake giggles. It amazed Iris how some women could casually hold a conversation with a man and not be intimidated. Too bad she wasn't one of them. When talking about legal matters, she was fine, but talking to them on a social level was another story. Occasionally, she could string two sentences together without stumbling over her words.

Iris watched as Nash studied the awards and photos on the wall above the glass case while Stacey studied him.

"That's a photo of what the facility looked like when we first opened." Stacey reached across Nash to point to the large photo of the mayor cutting the red ribbon. "As you can see, we've come a long way."

Nash nodded, not seeming to notice Stacey's body rubbed up against his or how her breasts were thrust in his face.

"I have to say, Nash…" Stacey paused and placed her hand on his arm. "May I call you Nash?"

He shrugged. "Sure."

"I saw your profile in the 'Most Eligible Bachelors' feature of *Essence* a few months ago. You're more handsome in person than you were in the magazine." She flipped her long red hair over her shoulder and stuck out her chest, her low-cut shirt accentuating her assets.

"Thanks."

Nash's disinterested glance didn't deter Stacey. "Since you're here, what do you think of having your photo taken for our celebrity wall?"

Appearing bored, Nash glanced over Stacey's shoulder at Iris. Suddenly, his hazel eyes sparkled with merriment and his easy smile sent a jolt of awareness to her gut. He stepped around Stacey and moved back to where Iris stood, snaking his arm around her waist possessively and hugging her close.

"Actually, Stacey, maybe some other time." He gave Iris a little squeeze and she gazed up at him, not missing his reassuring smile. "I have a hot date with a beautiful woman and I've kept her waiting long enough."

Stacey looked from Nash to Iris and then back at Nash. "So why are you here with Iris?" she cracked, and laughed at her own joke before waving it off. "I'm just kidding," she said drily. "But before you run off, Nash, maybe I can show you around and tell you more about our program."

Iris had never fought over a man, but at the moment she wanted to yank this woman's hair out. If she didn't put Stacey in her place now, there was no telling what else the woman would offer Nash.

"Thanks, Stacey, but I've got this," Iris said and found Nash's hand. She didn't miss the mischievous grin that spread across his face when she interlocked her fingers with his. "You ready?" she asked him.

"Ready when you are, sweetheart."

Iris felt a mixture of elation and nervousness as she walked off with Nash. She knew pretending that she and Nash were an item was a bit high-school-ish, but damn if it didn't feel good to leave Stacey standing there with her mouth hanging open.

Nash walked alongside Iris as she showed him the computer and art rooms, giving him information about the various programs the center offered. She told him about their process for recruiting volunteers, as well as the goal to raise $1.5 million in the next three years.

"In here is the gymnasium," Iris said and pointed to the double doors, each of which had had a small rectangular glass installed in it. Nash opened the door, allowing her to enter first. "This recreation space was awful when I first started volunteering, but it went through a much-needed renovation this past winter, thanks to several grants. The floor and ceiling were redone, bleachers installed, and all new lighting was added."

Nash nodded. "Very nicely done." He jogged over to a rack of basketballs and started dribbling one. "Does the center have any sports programs?"

She watched him make a few baskets. Her heart rate kicked up a notch as his bicep muscles bulged with every move he made.

"Uh, yep, it does," she stammered. It was hard to focus when his muscular arms had her full attention. *Shoot, what was I talking about? Oh, yeah...*

"Yep, it does. Soccer, football, baseball and basketball. But not only that, a few pro athletes from each of those sports come in each summer and host sport camps."

"That's cool. Tania used to attend a basketball camp when we lived in L.A., but outside of playing basketball for her school, she hasn't shown an interest in attending any camps in Atlanta." Nash dribbled the ball. "Do you play?" he asked, holding up the basketball.

"I used to."

"How about a little one-on-one?" He shot the ball from the three-point line and made it. He then followed that with an easy layup.

Iris had played basketball in high school and received an athletic scholarship to attend Spelman College, but hadn't played ball much since then. She knew she could hold her own against Nash, but basketball was a contact sport, and too much of that with him probably wouldn't be a good idea. As it was, she could barely breathe whenever he was close, and the way he made a simple touch feel like a sensual caress sent brazen thoughts straight to her brain.

"So, what do you say?" Nash continued shooting around, making one basket after another.

"About what?"

"About playing. How about a game?"

"I don't know, Nash. You clearly play often and I don't want to embarrass myself."

"I play, but not often. I'm sure you'll do fine. Besides, it's just me and we'll just be playing around for fun."

She pulled her bottom lip between her teeth and thought about it for a few seconds. "Oh, what the heck, why not?"

Iris sat her bag on the bottom bleacher. She removed her sweater and tossed it next to the bag, leaving her with a white T-shirt and jeans on.

Nash threw her the ball. "Let's play to eleven, counting by ones." He tugged his shirt out of his pants and lifted it over his head.

Iris was sure her heart stopped at that moment. She breathed in, trying to get oxygen to her lungs, but it wasn't working. Her head spun at the sight of his smooth, chiseled chest sprinkled with a light sheen of perspiration, his muscles contracting with every move. She tried not to stare, but she couldn't help it. His well-defined pecs were perfectly sculpted. She had always assumed he had an amazing body, but his flawless physique was way beyond her imagination.

"Uh, you can't play like that," she stuttered and the basketball slipped out of her hands and rolled a few feet away. She licked her lips and swallowed hard when Nash turned and faced her, giving her a better view of his enticing body.

"Play like what?" He frowned.

"Like…" She gestured at his body with a wave. "Like that. Put your shirt back on."

As realization of the problem dawned on Nash, he grinned and moved closer to Iris. Her heartbeat pounded in her ear and her stomach dropped when he made his pecs dance.

"Does my being half-naked bother you?"

Hell, yeah, it bothers me, she thought, but said nothing. She only continued to stare at the smoothness of his skin, appreciating how his broad shoulders tapered down to flat abs and a narrow waist.

"You know—" Nash yanked on one of her belt loops and pulled her closer, his mouth so close she could smell his fresh breath "—you could take off your shirt, too, if you feel that you're at a disadvantage. I won't mind."

Snapping out of her daze, Iris tilted her head and met his gaze. "Yeah, I bet you wouldn't." She pushed against his hard chest and regretted it when she felt his smooth and muscular body beneath her palms. There was no way she could play basketball with him and not be distracted by him.

Nash shrugged. "Oh, well, since you're not going to remove your T-shirt, let's get this game started." He swatted her behind before picking up the basketball.

"Hey! Keep your hands to yourself," she fussed, no real threat behind her words.

A friendly slap on the behind wasn't uncommon on the court, but when it was Nash doing the swatting, it felt a little too good for comfort.

"Make it take it," he said and threw her the ball, letting her know that if she made the basket, she would get to take the ball out of bounds.

Iris caught the ball and dribbled, using her body to protect the basketball from Nash. She turned and faked as if she was going to go up the court with the ball. When she did so, her body lunged in Nash's face, but instead she ducked and went under his arm, charging to the basket.

"Nice shot."

Iris took the basketball out of bounds and Nash tossed it back to her. "You know, if you decide to give up because I'm too much for you, I won't hold it against you."

Nash laughed. "Sweetheart, you're welcome to hold anything against me, especially this fine ass." He grabbed her butt with two hands and squeezed.

"Foul!" she screamed and lost the ball. She watched him charge to the basket and dunk, totally ignoring her protest.

"I never would have guessed you to be a trash talker, Counselor. I'm impressed, girl. You've got skills. Too bad I'm going to spank you out here."

"We'll see," Iris mumbled and hustled for the ball when it slipped out of his hands. Dribbling, she hunched over and backed him down the court. His arms and hands worked feverishly to steal the ball, his powerful body hovering over her, wreaking havoc on her senses. His hot breath against the damp skin of her neck sent scandalous prickles of desire up and down her spine. If he wanted to play dirty with no shirt, rubbing his body against her and screwing with her concentration, then two could play that game.

She put a little more booty into her dribble, bumping and wiggling against the front of his body, feeling his shaft swell against her butt. A small smile touched her lips when he groaned and cursed under his breath when she nudged him and went up for another shot. *Mmm, this might be fun after all.*

Nash didn't know how much more he could take. Her ass bumping against the front of his body was doing wicked things to his concentration. They'd been playing for the past fifteen minutes and, though he was winning, seven to five, he was impressed by her skills. The only problem was her luscious body thumping and rubbing against his. Each time she tried to steal the ball, her soft hands made contact with his chest or his stomach. At one point, she even brushed up against his package, and his body responded immediately. Hell, if he didn't know any better, he would think she was trying to entice him with her seductive dribbling and the full body contact that she considered guarding.

He went up for a layup and missed. He never did that, but playing against her today, he was missing shots he had once made with ease back when he was eight years old.

"Are you getting tired?" she taunted. "That's the third layup you've missed. I hope you're not trying to let me win. I can beat you on my own."

Funny how all of a sudden the shy, introverted defense attorney he wanted to know better was now threatening to beat him in basketball. Again, she dribbled the ball, her back to him and her ass bouncing against the front of his body.

"Come on, Mr. Hotshot. Show me what you've got."

"That's it!" he said in a low growl and slapped the ball from her hands. He pushed her up against the wall, careful not to hurt her.

"What…" she gasped, her breath coming in short spurts and her breasts heaving, which turned him on more.

Before she could breathe another word, he locked her arms above her head, silencing her protest when he lowered his mouth to hers, hungrily exploring the softness of her lips and the deliciousness of her taste. The full length of his body pressed into her and she moaned against his mouth. Nash had never wanted a woman as much as he wanted the one who was now molded against his body.

He released her arms from above her head and gripped her hips, grinding his erection against her. The sweet, intoxicating scent of her flowery fragrance assailed his nostrils. He couldn't get close enough with the barrier of their clothes currently restricting him from feeling all of her.

His tongue stroked the inner recesses of her mouth and she shivered against him, groaning and gripping his arms. She slowly slid her hands up his sweaty biceps and looped her arms around his neck, increasing the pressure of their kiss with a fervor that matched his. Desire vibrated through his veins and straight to his groin when her large breasts crushed against his bare chest.

"Do you feel what you do to me whenever I'm within a foot of you?" he mumbled against her lips, then pressed his erection against her body and moaned when she gripped his neck tighter.

His lips left hers and nibbled at her earlobe, then he worked his way down her scented neck. Everything within him wanted—no, needed—to be closer to her. She squirmed against him, only intensifying the flames that were roaring within his body. He recaptured her lips, more demandingly this time, and she moaned against his mouth when his hand cupped her breast, stroking and teasing. His blood sizzled and he marveled at how perfectly she fit into his hand. He tweaked a taut nipple through her thin T-shirt and she moved against his body uncontrollably, sending his need for her into overdrive.

He moved a hand back to her round butt and rubbed his pelvis against her over and over again, needing to feel more of her. Iris's whimper only fueled his craving to be inside her, but a voice in the back of his brain warned it was too soon. He'd surely scare her away if he did all he wanted to do to her at that moment. But still he couldn't stop his hips from rotating against her, the friction between them sparking a passion that was threatening to be released. Nash couldn't ever remember being so turned on by a woman, and almost to the point of no return, while still mostly clothed.

He palmed her butt, squeezing and rocking against her, loving the sounds coming from the back of her throat while he devoured her mouth. Iris arched her body, her nipples swollen against his bare chest. He knew he'd be a goner at any minute. Her breaths came in short spurts and her hands moved more frantically on his back as she flowed with the rhythm he'd started, her moves threatening to take him over the edge.

"Nash," she whimpered.

To hell with it. He needed to feel all of her. Without breaking contact, he went for her belt buckle, anxiously loosening it. She cried his name more breathlessly and he sensed she was nearing her release. He let go of her belt and increased his pace, wishing he were inside her rather than bumping and grinding like two teenagers. But hell, he was barely hanging on and couldn't stop even if he wanted to.

Iris tore her lips from his. "Nash!" she cried out, her eyes shut tight and her head thrashing back and forth while her nails clawed into his bare shoulders. A strangled scream swooshed through her lips. He silenced her, covering her mouth roughly with his as waves of ecstasy roared through him. Her body shook and trembled, hammering against him. Within seconds, a low growl tore from his throat, and his body convulsed and jerked viciously as his own release rocked him to the core.

Nash fought to get control, his heartbeat pounding double-time. Panting, he wrapped his arm around Iris's waist, placing his other arm against the wall, holding them both up. This…whatever the hell they had just done…was the most intense experience he'd had in a long time. Too tired to speak, he just held her, loving how good she felt in his arms.

Still trying to catch his breath, he placed a light kiss alongside Iris's temple. Her head lay against his bare chest and her hands heavily gripped his back belt loops. He knew what it meant to be weak in the knees. Right now, he could barely stand and it didn't help that his damp briefs were plastered against him. If he didn't think it would freak Iris out, he would laugh. Though he wasn't a stranger to living his life on the edge, this was definitely a first.

He glanced down at Iris. She had surprised the hell out of him. Never in a million years would he have expected this amount of passion from her, which made him want her that much more.

And hot damn...she's a screamer.

Chapter 7

Iris had collapsed against Nash's sweaty chest, not believing what they had just done. In all of her thirty-four years, she would have never thought she was capable of something so lasciviously erotic. And in a public gym, no less. *Oh, my God, what was I thinking?* A shiver skittered down the length of her body when her mind wandered to the memory of her orgasm. Her release, both exhilarating and mind-numbing, was so over the top she thought her heart would jump out of her chest. *Okay, so I wasn't thinking...I was feeling.*

She snuggled closer, her arms wrapped around his narrow waist, not caring that they both were a sweaty, wet mess. They'd been standing in the same spot for the past few minutes, while aftershocks were still fluttering within her and her mind was still trying to comprehend how they ended up in each other's arms. "Don't think, just be," Janna often said. Iris sighed with pleasant exhaustion. The wildest part in all of this was that she felt no shame.

A door to the gym opened and then closed, but for the life of her she was unable to move. It wasn't because Nash had her pinned to the wall. It was because she didn't want to move.

Iris startled when someone behind them cleared their throat. Nash didn't move, except to place a kiss against her temple as if he could care less about who had intruded on their intimate moment.

Iris lifted her head and glanced over Nash's shoulder. *Oh, great. Stacey.*

"Sorry to interrupt, but I didn't want to leave before saying goodbye to Nash."

Iris leaned back from Nash without removing her arms from around his waist. He met her gaze. "Is she serious?" he mumbled, his voice huskier than usual.

Iris almost burst out laughing at the face he made, but she held herself in check and nodded. With Nash as her cover, she hurried and stuffed her shirt into her pants and fastened her belt.

Without moving one hand from the wall or the other that held her in place, Nash looked over his shoulder. "Goodbye, Stacey."

Not to be ignored, Stacey said, "I see you're a little busy, Nash, but I was wondering if maybe you would like to go out sometime?"

Iris's mouth dropped open and her heart pounded hard against her rib cage. Here Nash was, half-dressed and with her pinned against the wall, yet Little Miss Redhead had the nerve to ask him out? Who the heck did that? The more Iris thought about it, the more indignant she became. It was going to take a few linebackers to keep her from tackling Stacey.

Iris attempted to step around Nash to handle this woman once and for all, but he tightened his grip around her waist, cementing her in place.

"Relax," he whispered against her lips. Without taking his eyes from Iris, he said, "No, thanks, Stacey. All of my free time will be consumed by Iris."

The next morning, Iris stared off into space, her spoon clanking against the inside of her cereal bowl. Her second week of "vacation" was off to a good start thanks to Nash. Their *date* the night before was one she wouldn't forget. She couldn't ever remember enjoying herself so much with a man. Showing him around the center, playing basketball in the new gym and… Heat spread through her body at the thought of what they had done in the gym…against the wall. Her explosive orgasm spoke volumes of Nash's ability to turn her on and take her to a point of no return. Even now, just thinking about his hands on her body, his lips against her lips, and the way he…

"You might want to get another bowl of cereal. I don't think coffee and cereal go *that* well together," Iris heard Tania say.

Iris glanced up, surprised to find Janna and Tania standing in the kitchen. "Hey," she said, and then gasped when she looked down at her bowl of cereal. "Oh, my God, what is wrong with me?" Her cereal swam in coffee instead of milk.

"You must have had a helluva night, sis," Janna teased, laughing as she strolled over to the refrigerator and grabbed a bottle of water.

Iris narrowed her eyes at her sister, daring her to continue.

"*Sooo,* you came in kind of late. Did you get your..." She paused and glanced over her shoulder. "Cover your ears, Tania. Better yet, go to your room."

"Why?" Tania frowned.

"Go!"

"Aw, come on, Janna. It's not like I don't know what Iris and Uncle Nash did last night."

"Girrrl!" Janna chuckled and Tania giggled as she bolted out of the room with Janna chasing behind her.

Horrified, Iris covered her face with her hands. Tania had known that she and Nash met at the community center to work on the bookcases, but Iris wondered what else Tania thought she knew.

Janna hurried back into the kitchen and sat on the barstool next to Iris. "You got some, didn't you?" she whispered conspiratorially. "I want to know everything. Well, maybe not *everything,* but I want some details. And don't try to deny it because I saw that lovesick puppy-dog look in your eyes. As if the coffee in your cereal wasn't enough."

Iris covered her face with her hands and groaned. Could people really tell just by looking at her what she had done and how she felt?

"I need some water," she mumbled and shot out of her seat. With shaky hands, she grabbed a glass from the cabinet and knocked over a couple cups that tumbled out.

Janna almost fell off the stool while laughing. "Dang, girl, was he that good? He's got you in here blushing, you're flustered *and* you've screwed up your breakfast."

"Stop… It wasn't like that." Iris poured a glass of water, careful not to cause any other catastrophes, and reclaimed her seat. She took a sip of the ice-cold liquid and sighed. "We hung out at the community center for a few hours and then we went out to eat."

"And then?"

"And then I came home and went to bed…alone." Technically, she had been alone, but in her dreams, Nash was sharing her bed and doing unthinkable things to her body. Her cheeks burned. Lying beside her, he had stared down at her naked form, his hazel eyes burning a path from her kiss-swollen lips down to the tips of her manicured toes. She had shuddered when his desire-laden gaze ignited her blood, and her body heated without even being touched. How was it possible that a simple look—in a dream, no less—could have her dangling on the edge of control?

In her mind, he had lowered his mouth over hers and hungrily devoured her lips, his tongue stroking hers until a groan rose from her throat. His hand was skimming over her breasts, tweaking and fondling the hardened buds before settling over her stomach. Instinctively, her body had arched against his cool hand when he had slid it down to the opening between her thighs, his fingers teasing the wisp of hair covering her mound. Her heart thundered and she moaned against his mouth, as her legs opened wider for his fingers to explore.

"Nash," she whispered.

"Iris," her sister called out several times, then slapped her hand against the countertop. "Iris!"

Iris jumped. "What?"

Janna studied her with a critical squint. Iris tried to

ignore her unwavering gaze, especially since she wasn't sure if she had actually called Nash's name out loud. What she really wanted to do was tell her sister everything, every tongue-tangling, toe-curling, bumping-and-grinding thing that happened yesterday. Instead, she lifted her glass to her lips and gulped down her water.

"Well, you and Nash did something. Though you're acting weird this morning, you actually look rested… and you're damn near glowing." Janna eased off the barstool and grabbed her large handbag from a nearby chair. She headed out of the kitchen, but stopped short and glanced over her shoulder. "Whatever he did to you, or for you, tell him that I said to do it again."

A sweet, soulful melody flowed through Nash's lips while he pulled his saxophone case from the trunk of his car and whistled as he sauntered into Platinum Pieces–Midtown. He knew the house band would be rehearsing later and decided to do a few numbers with them before their set tonight.

Nash entered his office and was surprised to find Nigel sitting behind his desk, talking on his cell phone.

"It sounds like someone's happy," his friend said when he hung up. "You're whistling and you have your sax case. I can't remember the last time I've seen you so…so, oh, I don't know, happy. What happened? Did you hit the lottery or something?"

A vision of Iris flowed to the forefront of his mind. "Almost." He couldn't remember the last time he'd enjoyed being with a woman as much as he liked hanging out with Iris. And though he had mixed feelings about the incident in the gym, they were combustible together, even with their clothes on. He had no doubt their lovemaking would be just as explosive if they ever hit the sheets.

Nash sat his briefcase and sax next to the sofa. "What are you doing here so early in the morning? It's not even seven-thirty."

"Remember, we changed the meeting to eight instead of twelve-thirty. I figured I'd come here and take care of a few things while I waited for you, instead of going downtown to Dupree Enterprises and then having to stop and come back here.

"That makes sense." Nash started the coffeemaker that sat in the corner of his office on the built-in credenza.

"What did you get into yesterday? I tried calling you, but kept getting your voice mail. Speaking of which—" he pulled his cell phone from his pocket "—I need to email Luke about the photo shoot for the new club in Buckhead." He glanced up. "Sorry about that. What were you going to say?"

"I hung out at this community center down near College Park, played some b-ball—" he shrugged "—and messed around a little before heading home."

"Man, you should've called me. I haven't played ball in a couple of months. Who'd you play with, anyway?" Nigel glanced at him and then went back to typing something into his phone. "And why'd you go down south when we usually play at the fitness center?"

To Nigel, anything south of downtown Atlanta was considered *down south.*

Nash toyed with the saxophone paperweight sitting on his desk, a gift from his housekeeper when he opened his first nightclub in Los Angeles. "I played with Iris Sinclair."

Nigel stopped fiddling with his phone and gave Nash his full attention. "Iris? Iris, as in the *hot* defense attorney who's taking care of your kid? That Iris?"

Nash nodded. "That would be the one. She finally agreed to go out with me, but only if she planned our date. We met up at Mercy Youth Community Center, where she does volunteer work." Nash scooted down in his seat and rested his head against the back of the chair. "She wanted me to help her assemble bookshelves."

A flashback of him pinning Iris to the wall, dry-humping her like a damned dog in heat, blazed through his mind. He had been so caught up in the moment that he didn't think. She wasn't like the other women he dated. Iris was special. Yet he had treated her like a quick lay, not taking into consideration where they were, how she felt about him or how she'd feel after the fact. To his surprise, she hadn't seemed bothered by the experience at all. If anything, it had loosened her up and she let down her guard.

Nigel propped his elbows on the desk and interlocked his fingers. "Let me get this straight. You asked out the woman…the woman who has agreed to care for your child over the next couple of months in order to keep her out of foster care? Man, what were you thinking?"

Nash sat up and glared at his friend. "What do you mean, what was I thinking? She's an amazing woman. Why shouldn't I have asked her out?"

Nigel slammed his palms against the desk. "Come on, Nash, you know your track record with women.

The last thing you need is to get involved with this woman, break her heart and risk Tania being sent to a foster home."

"It's not like that... Iris is different." Nash leaned forward, rubbing his forehead. True, he didn't have the best history with women, but he'd never been with a woman like Iris. "I can't explain it, Nigel, but I really like this woman."

"You really liked them all. How can you possibly—"

"I know what I like." Nash stood and moved around the room. "Iris is not like the other women I've gone out with. She's real, man. She's not caught up with what I have, or trying to trap me into marriage, nor is she concerned about what I can do for her. Heck, after leaving the community center, she even chose to have dinner at the Waffle House instead of some expensive five-star restaurant.

"Still..."

"Nigel, she's amazing. She's as beautiful on the inside as she is on the outside, and she genuinely cares about people. I have too much respect for her to do anything that would hurt her. But that's all beside the point. I'm still getting to know her and I don't even know if she'll go out with me on a real date. So this whole conversation might be a moot point."

Nash respected his friend's opinion. They were closer than most brothers and shared their opinions of the other's actions, whether solicited or not. He knew Nigel meant well, and it wasn't that Nash himself hadn't thought about the ramifications of getting involved with Iris; it was that he couldn't help himself. He was drawn to her like a magnet to a steel beam.

Nigel stood, shaking his head. He eased around the

desk, his hands shoved into his pockets. "I don't know, Nash. I think you're taking a big risk in pursuing her."

Nash hunched his shoulders. "You know me. I'm Mr. Risk-Taker. I might not be looking for anything serious right now, but I'd like to get to know Iris better. She's good people."

"That's just it. She doesn't come across as a woman who'll partake in one of your noncommittal affairs. You said it yourself, she's not like the others. From what I've read and heard about her, I bet she has too much respect for herself to get involved seriously with the likes of you."

Nash's eyebrows drew together. "What the hell is that supposed to mean?"

"It means you're not the marrying type, but she is. Like Picasso once said, 'There are only two types of women—goddesses and doormats.' Iris is definitely not in the latter category. If you're not looking for anything serious, you should leave her the hell alone."

I would leave her alone if I could stop thinking about her.

Chapter 8

Iris pulled her Mercedes C63 AMG onto the grounds of the private school Tania attended and fell in line behind the other luxury vehicles. Kids hurried out of cars, some even before their parents came to a complete stop. No doubt they were trying to get away before Mom planted an embarrassing kiss on their cheeks.

"Okay, so your uncle is going to pick you up after school and drop you at the apartment. I might not be there, but Janna will be there."

Tania sighed. "You do know that I'm not a little kid, right? You don't have to make sure someone is there when I get out of school. I have a key."

Iris tried not to laugh at the incredulous look Tania gave her. She, too, remembered the days of feeling as if Mama Adel treated her like a baby, preparing her lunch and some days walking with her to the bus stop.

"I know, I know, but I want to know someone is there to greet you when you get home from school. You probably don't appreciate this right now, but when you get to be my age, you're going to look back and remember how good it felt for someone to greet you at the door."

Tania shook her head and smiled. She reached for the door handle, but stopped and turned back to Iris, her expression serious. "Uncle Nash told me about your date yesterday and how much he likes you," she started, then glanced outside before returning her attention to Iris. "Just so you know, I'm cool with you guys hooking up. I actually think he needs someone like you."

Before Iris could respond, Tania kissed her on the cheek and bolted from the car. She didn't know how long she sat stunned before the blaring of a horn from behind her shook her out of her reverie. She pulled away from the curb, her heart melting at the thought of Tania's feelings toward her. Iris couldn't believe how attached she was getting to Tania. It had only been a couple of weeks and already she wasn't looking forward to the day Tania went back home to Nash.

When she exited the school's property, her cell phone rang.

"Hello."

"Good morning, Iris."

Good Lord. Iris shivered. The deep timbre of Nash's hypnotic voice sent shock waves of desire to every cell in her body and made her want to climb through the phone and throw herself at him.

"Good morning," she finally said, hoping her voice was steadier than she felt.

"I was wondering if you would join me at the new club for breakfast this morning."

The invitation was tempting, especially since she had ruined her bowl of cereal earlier. Besides, not only was she curious about the new club, she also wanted to see Nash. That last thought both thrilled and terrified her. Being with him was equivalent to being on a roller-coaster ride, sitting at the top of the highest point and anticipating the thrill of roaring down the hill, her hair blowing in the wind, her screams piercing the air.

"It's just breakfast," he said to her silence. "I assure you my intentions are honorable. Besides, a couple of weeks ago you said you were willing to do anything it takes to keep Tania and me together. This is about her. I want your opinion on a few things."

Iris twisted her mouth and scrunched up her face, wondering if this was a trick. She admired his persistence. This was the third or fourth time he had asked her out since that evening she'd had dinner with him, Tania and Ms. Dalton at their home. Despite what he had told Stacey, she honestly thought that yesterday would have been their only date. *Come on, Iris, live a little. It's just breakfast.* She could hear Janna's voice in her head. But Janna didn't know that a simple outing for her and Nash could easily turn into something much steamier. Case in point—their basketball game yesterday.

"Okay, when?" she finally asked.

"Are you cooking enough for me, too?" A familiar voice rang through Platinum Pieces–Buckhead's soon-to-be state-of-the-art commercial kitchen. "Mr.

Big-Time, working eighty-hour weeks, I didn't know you still made time for cooking."

Ace Hardison, an ex-boxer and another of Nash's longtime friends from Compton, was the head bouncer for Nash's midtown nightclub. Soon, he would be head of security for both locations.

"I cook periodically, but not often. Except this woman is special." Nash turned to Ace. He had actually been surprised that she accepted his invite, but it didn't matter. This morning, he hadn't planned on taking no for an answer. There was something about Iris that piqued his interest, and he intended to find out what that something was.

When he and his twin brother were younger, their father taught them how to cook, claiming it to be the best way to a woman's heart. Nash's parents were avid foodies. Growing up, not only had he learned to cook, but Nash had experienced every type of cuisine. Whatever recipe his mother was trying out, her sons were her number-one guinea pigs.

Nash hadn't cooked for a woman in years, having never felt the desire to do so. But this morning, he woke up thinking about Iris and the idea popped into his head after his meeting with Nigel.

"I'll check back with you later to let you know what I find out about the cameras in the parking lot. I'm not sure why they're not working. But for now, let me head out before your woman gets here."

My woman. It had a nice ring to it, but he wasn't looking for anything serious. He just wanted to get to know her a little better.

"Sounds good," Nash said. They bumped fists before Ace headed to the rear of the building and out the back door.

Nash finished cutting the fruit and placed it near the place setting for two on the stainless-steel prep table with two barstools pushed up to it. It made a nice makeshift eating area, and the small bouquet of mixed flowers he had added softened the industrial feel of the space.

His phone beeped, letting him know he had a text message. He wiped his hands on his apron and glanced at his cell phone sitting on the counter.

I'm out front. He read Iris's message. Anxious to see her again, he headed to the front of the building.

"Hey," she said when he opened the door.

"Hey, yourself." Nash stood back to let her in and inhaled the fresh floral scent of her perfume. He admired how sexy she looked in her fitted red blouse, skinny jeans and short red heels. "You look great…and relaxed. I think vacation agrees with you."

She gave a nervous laugh. "Yeah, I've been enjoying this time off more than I thought I would. I'm even thinking about adding another week, giving me four weeks instead of three."

"You definitely have the right idea. I plan to take some time off once we get the doors open here." She followed him into the foyer, which opened onto a large dining area on the left and a semicircular bar to the right. "Why don't we eat and then I'll show you around?"

"That sounds fine." She stopped and glanced around the main dining area. "I can't believe the changes you've already made. This area is definitely bigger than I remember. I came here once for dinner when it was Simon's and it doesn't look like the same place."

"We've made a few changes. We're going for more of an open concept instead of chopping up the room." They moved along and he pointed out various features. "We added that stage. Since I've always loved music, I wanted to make sure we had a spot that could host live performances. There's also a smaller stage upstairs, which is where the VIP lounge will be."

"When are you scheduled to open? Looks like it'll be soon."

"We're surprisingly ahead of schedule."

"Oh, Nash, this is lovely," she said when she saw the makeshift table, her hand over her heart. "You didn't have to go through all of this trouble. I usually keep breakfast pretty simple, just toast and coffee."

"Well, since you're on vacation and have time for a real breakfast, how about cheesecake-mousse crepes with mixed berries, eggs, sausage and bacon? In addition to the fruit on the table, I also have chocolate-chip waffles."

"Mmm, crepes and chocolate chip waffles, a man after my own heart," she said in a wistful voice. Realizing what she just said, she dropped her hand and diverted her eyes. "Uh, I mean…I have a sweet tooth, also."

Nash laughed. Not wanting to embarrass her more, he said, "I threw the waffles on the menu at the last minute. I had a taste for them. It's good to know I'm not the only one who loves something sweet." He pulled out the stool for her. "Breakfast will be ready shortly."

"Wait a minute, you cooked?"

Nash feigned offense. "What? You think I'm all brains and brawn, and no skills?"

"I mean… I didn't mean to imply…"

Nash shook his head and laughed. "I'm just messing with you, Iris." He went to the refrigerator and pulled out a pitcher. "Is orange juice okay with you? I also made a pot of coffee."

"Orange juice would be great, and though I've met my coffee quota for today, maybe just a little would be good." She emphasized the amount by pinching her thumb and forefinger together.

As they talked like old friends throughout breakfast, Nash thought that if he was intrigued by this woman before, he definitely wanted to get to know her better now. *Beauty and brains.*

"You know, this past week without Tania at home, and wondering who set her up with the drugs has been like living a nightmare."

"I can only imagine," Iris said. "Well, if it makes you feel any better, she's doing fine, and Noelle will not stop until she gets to the bottom of who planted the drugs on Tania."

"I know. I have complete faith in your law firm. It's just that I never thought anything like this would happen to us. And don't even get me started about that judge."

"Juvie judges often recommend family counseling," Iris said, cutting into her waffle. "Some believe a child's bad behavior is brought on by something the child is missing from their parents, or by problems at home."

"When the judge *required* me and Tania to seek individual counseling first, I thought he was talking crazy." Nash chuckled and took a sip from his second cup of coffee. "But I can honestly say it hasn't been as bad as I thought it would be."

"Glad to hear that. Family counseling starts in a few weeks. Are you ready?"

Nash shrugged. "If it means getting Tania back home and our lives back on track, then yes. I'm ready." The only thing he wasn't ready for was not seeing Iris as often. With the setup they had now, he saw her daily, if only for a few minutes when he dropped Tania off after school.

"I'm going to miss her when she goes back home."

"Somehow, I don't think you're going to get rid of her that easy. She's as taken with you as you are with her. We both are."

Iris smiled and lowered her head. Her shyness was endearing, but it cracked Nash up how she could be shy and reserved one minute, and a formidable defense attorney the next. He had read up on some of her most recent cases and to say he was impressed would be an understatement. She had won her last fifteen cases. In an interview she had done, she attributed the wins to having an amazing defense team, but from what Nash knew of her, he was sure she had had a huge hand in the wins.

He topped his coffee cup off and then held the pot up to ask Iris if she'd like more. When she shook her head no, he asked, "So, what made you go into criminal law?"

Iris hesitated. She wiped her mouth with the cloth napkin and laid it on the table. "My biological mother."

"Was she a lawyer?"

Iris chuckled. "No, but she was definitely a force to

be reckoned with. She didn't take mess from anyone. Mom was a high-school English teacher."

"Teacher…lawyer, I don't get it."

"When I was fourteen, my mother was shot by a teen who took a gun to school because he was being bullied."

"Oh, my God, Iris, I'm sorry." Nash covered her hand with his and squeezed.

"It's okay. I came to terms with her death years ago. She died doing something she cared about—taking care of *her* kids, as she used to refer to them." Iris smiled. "The way she talked about her students, you would've thought I had siblings."

"So what happened?" Nash released her hand, but rolled his stool closer.

"The student thought that if he brought a gun to school, he could scare the kid who was bullying him." She stopped and blew out a breath. "Things got heated in the classroom, but my mother was able to talk him out of hurting anyone. He eventually handed her the gun, but it went off and she was shot in the chest. She died immediately."

"Oh, baby, I'm so sorry." Nash wrapped his arms around Iris, placing a light kiss against her temple. "We don't have to talk about this if you don't want."

She shook her head, but didn't move out of his arms. "It's okay. My mother and that kid are the reasons I became a lawyer." She toyed with the hem of her napkin. "He went to prison, though he claimed he was only trying to scare the kids who were bullying him. He hadn't intended on hurting anyone. I believed him."

"Really?"

"Don't get me wrong, I was heartbroken that my

mother was killed, but I could relate to what that kid was going through. I wanted to kill bullies lots of times who made fun of my dark skin and my height."

Nash rubbed her back, shocked to hear Iris say anything about killing.

"It's just by the grace of God that I never did." She released a weary breath. "As I got older, and some of the anger subsided, I didn't think the kid who shot my mother should spend the rest of his life in prison. I had heard that his parents couldn't afford a lawyer, so he was assigned a public defender who didn't represent him well."

"And that's why most of your clients are teens."

Iris nodded.

Nash didn't know what to say. She had not only lost her mother at a young age, but she had had to endure bullying, as well. Yet she was gorgeous and one of the sweetest people he'd ever met. The thought of someone picking on her was crazy.

Iris leaned back without pulling completely out of his arms and met his gaze. "I didn't mean to ruin this wonderful breakfast you've made with such a heavy story."

"Don't apologize. I'm glad you told me."

Several synchronized beeps pierced the air and Iris scurried away from him in search of her purse, which she found on the bottom shelf of the prepping table.

"Oh, crap, Macy's going to kill me." Iris plucked her cell phone from her handbag. "That's my reminder alarm. I'm supposed to meet her at the gym in ten minutes." She glanced at her watch. "I'm sure it's going to take at least twenty to get there."

She placed her phone back in her purse and started gathering dishes.

"Leave it." Nash halted her. "I'll take care of those. You go ahead. I'm glad you came by on such short notice."

Iris twisted her mouth and frowned at the mound of dishes. "I hate to leave like this, especially since you were kind enough to prepare such a wonderful breakfast."

"Don't worry about it. I'll have this cleaned up in no time."

"Okay, well, if you're sure." Nash took her hand and they walked toward the front of the building. "I would offer to reciprocate by preparing you breakfast one morning, but that wouldn't be a good idea."

"Why not?" Nash slowed.

She hesitated. "Uh, I can't cook."

Nash let out a hearty laugh. He thought for sure she was going to say something about not being able to see him because of Tania, or the case, or because of his reputation. It was hard to believe she couldn't cook.

Iris swatted his arm. "It's not *that* funny."

"Actually, it is," he said, still chuckling. He pulled her into his arms. Staring into her eyes, his tongue traced the soft fullness of her lips. He captured first her top lip, then her bottom lip, gently between his teeth. "I love kissing you."

Her phone beeped.

"I really have to go," she said, but didn't move out of his arms.

"Have dinner with me one night this week. I want to take you on a real date." When she opened her mouth to speak, he placed his finger against her lips. "And before you come up with a reason for why you can't, let me remind you of how much fun we've had together these past couple of days."

He hadn't brought up their basketball game, not wanting to embarrass her, but he had no intention of letting her avoid him. They had a connection and he wanted to see where it would lead.

"I'd love to have dinner with you."

Iris hurried to the gym's locker room and did a quick change. She was scheduled to meet Macy twenty minutes ago and had no doubt her sister would harass her for being late, especially since Macy had to get back to work.

"Girl, where have you been? I had to give this woman the evil eye when she tried to use that machine," Macy said, eyeing the elliptical next to her. "You're never late."

Iris climbed onto the machine. "I am so sorry. I had an impromptu breakfast meeting and lost track of time."

Macy took in Iris's appearance. "You look…great. And based on the head turns you received on your way over here, I'd say that I'm not the only one who has noticed."

Iris peered to her left and met the gaze of a man she'd seen in the gym numerous times. He smiled and she returned the gesture. Though she'd seen him often, this was the first time he'd paid her any attention.

"Are you using a different makeup or something? You're glowing, and I noticed you have a little extra pep in your step today."

"Yeah, right."

"I'm serious. You seem…cheerful. What have you been up to? Who'd you have breakfast with? You're supposed to be on vacation. I hope you're not doing any work."

"Oh, no, it's nothing like that. I got together with Nash."

Macy hesitated. "Hmm, two days in a row. I called you yesterday and Janna told me you were out with Nash," she said in response to Iris's questioning gaze. "So, what do you think of him?"

Good question, Iris thought. Her feelings for Nash were all over the place. "He's not what I expected. Janna was right. He's really a nice guy. Charming, funny, brilliant. It's no wonder he's so successful. The way this man's mind works is so different from other men I've talked to. I was telling him about some of the challenges the center is having with meeting its financial goals, and within seconds he gave me numerous ideas."

Nash had so many more qualities that she liked. The way he made her feel at ease with little or no effort. The way he kissed, and the way he lit her body on fire with just a touch. She thought better of sharing those attributes with her sister.

"Sounds like you really like him."

"I do, and it doesn't hurt that he's easy on the eyes. Oh, and did I mention he can cook?" That last part had surprised Iris. The last thing she expected was for him to be a culinary genius.

"So, how do you know he can cook?"

She hesitated. "He prepared breakfast for me this morning."

"Iris, please tell me that you didn't spend the night

with that man," her sister said. "You've only known him a couple of weeks."

"Come on, Macy, you know good and well I didn't spend the night with him." *But I think I would've had he asked.* Iris shook her head to free herself of the lustful thought.

"He asked me out again," she said, increasing the resistance on the elliptical. With all of the calories she took in this morning, it was going to take an extra thirty minutes of cardio to make them disappear.

"Do you think it's a good idea to date Nash?"

Macy, always the voice of reason, was quick to pull her away from any idea until she evaluated the pros and cons. But this was one situation where Iris didn't want to hear it, especially now that she had decided to live a little.

"Macy, don't make more out of this than it is. We're just hanging out."

"That's how it starts, Iris. He's all charming and fun to hang out with now, but what about when you fall in love with him?"

"What? Who said anything about falling in love? We assembled bookshelves yesterday and ate breakfast today. Love never came up in the conversation."

"Don't get cute. You know what I mean. That man has the ability to break your heart, and from what I've heard, he's been breaking a few hearts lately."

Iris knew Nash was no choirboy, but as far as she was concerned, he'd been nothing but a gentleman. The scene in the gym came to mind. *But that was different,* Iris told herself. Yesterday, she hadn't wanted him to be a gentleman.

"I understand you like him, but I don't think it's a good idea to go out with him."

"A couple of weeks ago when we saw him at the restaurant, you and Janna were the ones who suggested I go out with him."

Macy said nothing.

"Now all of a sudden, he's too much of a ladies' man?" Iris lowered her voice when she noticed other gym members looking her way. "Macy, I'm a grown woman. Yes, there was a time I counted on you to fight my battles, but this is not one of them."

"Fine, do what you want." Macy stepped off the machine and wiped it down. "When he breaks your heart, don't come running to me."

"Mace..." Iris called after her and cursed under her breath when Macy kept walking. Luckily for Iris, her sister rarely stayed mad long. She'd catch up with her later and make things right.

Chapter 9

"Well, there's the superstar," Noelle said when Iris walked into her office and sat across from her at the small conference table. "Looks like you've been busy over the past five weeks."

"What do you mean?"

Iris glanced at the interior page of the tabloid newspaper that Noelle slid across the table. "Who Is the Tall Beauty With Nash Dupree?" She read the big bold letters across the top of the page and her heart sank. The photo was great and she had to admit that she and Nash made a nice-looking couple. But the timing was all wrong.

Iris wondered who else had seen the issue. She and Nash had gone on several dates in the weeks since their breakfast rendezvous. They had attended a movie premiere one night, where many photos had been taken.

Never would she have guessed that a shot of them would end up in one of these publications.

"Care to explain what's going on?"

Iris's gaze went back to the newspaper in front of her. She knew enough to know that though Nash and Tania weren't technically her clients anymore, it didn't look good that she was spending so much time with Nash. Thankfully, the news about Tania's arrest hadn't gone public. If it had, then it would really look bad for the firm.

"Hmm, you have nothing to say?" Noelle retrieved the paper, folded it and set it aside. "Tell me what's going on. I didn't hear from you during your vacation, and you've been back at work for two weeks and not once have you mentioned having an affair with Nash."

"Technically, we're not having an affair. We hang out sometimes." She shrugged. "That photo happened to be taken at a movie premiere a week or so ago. We went as friends."

"Well, as your friend, I say, get yours, girl! *But* as the attorney for Tania, who happens to be living with you because the courts think her uncle is unfit, I have to tell you that I don't know if your seeing Nash on a social level is a good idea. He and Tania are going through court-ordered therapy, trying to get their lives together. You don't want to stand in the way of his regaining custody of her. He might just come off as an even bigger playboy who snared his niece's former lawyer. Now I'm not saying that can't be done with you in the picture—no pun intended—but do you want to take that risk?"

In the back of Iris's mind, she knew her involvement with Nash wasn't a good idea, but she couldn't help herself when it came to him. Over the past month, she, Tania and Nash had attended events as a family, and Iris had fit well into their dynamic. And the times Iris spent with Nash alone were priceless. The intimate dinners, the toe-curling kisses and those sexually charged moments that made her want to throw all caution to the wind were hard to ignore.

"Pretend I was in your shoes. What would you tell me to do?" Noelle asked.

Iris put her elbows on the table and rested her head in her hands. "I would probably tell you to lay low from Nash until all of this is cleared up," Iris mumbled, hating that she knew she'd have to put the brakes on seeing him.

"Iris, honey, I'd be the first to admit that I'm glad to see you so happy. It's been a long time since I've seen this side of you. Lately, on most days, you're out of here by six." She unfolded the newspaper. "I think you and Mr. Dupree make a striking couple."

Iris gave her friend a weak smile, knowing it wasn't going to be easy to stop seeing Nash, but she didn't have a choice. She didn't want anything to keep him from getting Tania back.

"I'm going to do my best to wrap up Tania's case, and then appeal to the presiding judge. Hopefully, that'll mean that you and Nash won't have to be apart for too long."

Nash needed to get up.

The pitter-patter of rain tapped against his bedroom windows and lulled him into an unmotivated state, making him want to lounge around awhile longer. But he didn't have that luxury. There was work to do.

He eased out of bed and headed to the shower. The notion that he could take a nap in the middle of the afternoon and not be inundated with thoughts of Iris had turned out to be a joke. For a man who wasn't looking for a serious relationship, he sure was craving some time with her. The last time he saw her was the day the photo of them showed up in the tabloids. Since then, missing her had affected every aspect of his life, which was a first for him. Never had he been as enthralled by a woman as he was with Iris. Everything about her intrigued him, from her shyness to the way she responded to his kisses and his touch. He swallowed hard, thinking about the night of the movie premiere. He wanted to make love to her so badly that night he physically ached, but it was too soon. Her body's responses to him had said she was ready, but he could feel her emotionally holding back.

"How was your siesta?" Ms. Dalton asked Nash half an hour later when he walked into the kitchen.

"It was all right." He grabbed a mug from the cabinet and poured a cup of coffee from the carafe. "It started as a great idea, but I didn't get much sleep."

"No? Why not? Is something bothering you?"

"Nothing I can't handle." Or so he kept telling himself. His focus should be on getting Tania back home and getting Platinum Pieces–Buckhead open, but instead he was dwelling on his last conversation with Iris.

I really like you, Nash, but it doesn't look good for us to be spending so much time together. You should be keeping a low profile until this situation with you and Tania is settled in the courts.

The conversation should have made him happy, since he wasn't looking to get romantically involved with anyone. Instead, he was frustrated, mainly with himself. Sure, he didn't want anything serious with Iris, but there was just something about her that made him want to explore the startling connection they had. It didn't help that the three of them spending so much time together had felt like a family. Something he hadn't really thought much about having.

Nash glanced at his watch. He had thirty minutes before he had to pick Tania up from school.

"Oh, I forgot to tell you, Tania called and said Iris's sister Macy is picking her up today. Something about a science project."

Nash wondered if Iris was behind this little change in plans. Was this her way of continuing to avoid him? If he didn't pick Tania up from school and take her home, then there would be no chance of him running into Iris. This should have pleased him, but it didn't.

"Do you know if Tania called Iris?"

"I believe so." Ms. Dalton reached into the refrigerator and removed all items within her reach. It was time for her to scrub down the interior of the refrigerator. "I told Tania I would wake you, but she said she would call you later."

"I'm calling Iris." Nash glanced around the kitchen, looking for the cordless phone, sure it was lying on a counter nearby. "I want to know why Macy is picking up Tania when I always pick Tania up from school." A slow boil brewed within Nash. Just because Iris didn't want to see him didn't give her the right to keep him from Tania. Or at least that was the argument he was going with.

Ms. Dalton glanced over her shoulder. "I told you."

"Told me what?"

"That Macy is helping Tania with a science project." Wearing yellow latex gloves and holding a sponge, she backed away from the refrigerator. "What is going on with you? What happened between you and Iris?"

"What do you mean?"

"You know what I mean. Up until recently, Iris was the only thing you talked about. It was *Iris this* and *Iris that*. I've never heard you go on and on about a woman for as long as I can remember. So what changed?"

Nash grabbed an orange from the fruit basket on the counter and dropped into a seat at the breakfast bar. He rolled the fruit around in his hands for a few seconds, then peeled it while he debated on how much to tell Ms. Dalton.

"I don't know," he mumbled. "Apparently, it's best that I keep a low profile until this whole thing with the courts blows over." Nash popped a slice of orange into his mouth, savoring the sweet, juicy fruit. "In other words, no dating, and that includes not hanging out with Iris."

Ms. Dalton tossed the sponge into a small bucket and removed her gloves. "That's too bad. You two really seemed to hit it off. Why not just hang out, as you say, in less public places? Don't go to all of those fancy shindigs that you usually attend. I would hate for you to miss out on the best woman who has ever stepped into your life."

"I don't know." Nash finished off the orange and tossed the rind into the trash.

He thought about what Ms. Dalton said. Iris was like no other woman he'd ever met, but did he really want to pursue anything more with her? A small voice in the back of his mind said no, but then there was a louder voice that said yes.

He glanced at his watch again as he wiped down the counter. Since he didn't have to pick up Tania, he would head to Dupree Enterprises, the headquarters for his corporation. As an entrepreneur and investor, he owned numerous businesses and was always looking for his next big deal. Today, he and Nigel were planning to crunch some numbers. Nash had an opportunity to invest in a mid-level software company that was looking for an investor.

"Oh, and before you go to your office, can you stop by Iris's house and drop this basket off for Tania?" She gestured toward a large container sitting on the counter closest to the garage door.

Nash felt as if he'd just been given a gift. Now he didn't have to come up with an excuse to go by Iris's house.

"Sure, I can drop it off. What's in it?" He grabbed his car keys from the top of the refrigerator and made a move to lift the basket lid, but Ms. Dalton swatted his hand.

"Don't open that. It's for Tania."

"Well, what's in it?" Whatever it was smelled good enough for him to sneak a taste once he got in the car. He leaned a hip against the kitchen counter and folded his arms across his chest. "Why is it in a basket instead of a bag?"

Ms. Dalton sighed and furrowed her brow. "It's a picnic basket, boy, and it has some of Tania's favorite things in it. Since I'll be in L.A. for the next couple of weeks looking after my sister, I prepared a few treats for Tania."

"What about me? What am I supposed to eat while you're away?"

She patted his cheek the way she used to do when he was a kid. "You know I can't forget about my boy. You'll have lasagna, fried chicken, some cabbage and collard greens, and a few more dishes that I'll have left in the freezer. All you have to do is pop them into the microwave."

Nash could easily cook for himself, but he knew how much Ms. Dalton liked taking care of him and Tania. He couldn't imagine their lives without her.

"So, how long are you going to be gone again?"

"Two weeks."

"What time do you need me to take you to the airport in the morning?"

"My plane leaves at ten, but you know you don't have to drop me off. I can get a driver. That way you don't have to deal with that traffic."

"So you'll be ready around seven-thirty in the morning?" Nash asked as if she hadn't said anything about getting a car service. He grabbed the picnic basket and headed for the door. They had the same conversation every time she left town.

"Make it seven," she said, and went back to cleaning the refrigerator.

Iris sat in traffic along Peachtree Road, hating that there wasn't a better route to her penthouse. It didn't matter what time of day she traveled this stretch of road; traffic was always backed up.

"Come on, people! Why do we have to go through this every day?" she grumbled, exhausted from a long day at work. Her three-week vacation seemed like a distant memory. She'd been back at work for three weeks, but she had yet to fully catch up on everything, even after working at home late into the night. It didn't help matters that she was missing Nash.

Before Noelle had confronted her about her so-called *affair,* she and Nash had fallen into a nice routine, and the tag-team parenting was working with Tania. She'd drop Tania off at school most days and Nash picked her up. Iris was starting to enjoy their numerous impromptu family outings until she had to bring everything to a screeching halt. Still, there was one positive. Tania's grades had improved and there hadn't been any more complaints from her teachers regarding her behavior.

Iris inched her car forward as traffic crawled at a snail's pace in front of Lenox Mall. Though she liked living in Buckhead, and it was not too far from work, the area definitely had its disadvantages for evening commuters.

Her cell phone rang and Alicia Keys's voice permeated the interior of the car. Tania had set the ringtone to Keys's "Girl on Fire." Iris pushed the Bluetooth button on her steering wheel.

"Hi, Tania, what's up? Are you home yet?"

"Yes, I got here over an hour ago and was wondering when you'll be here."

Iris frowned. This was the third call in the past hour and a half asking about her whereabouts or when Iris would be home. These repeated messages had caused Iris to leave work at 6:00 p.m., instead of eight as she'd planned.

"What's going on, Tania?" Iris asked cautiously. "Is everything okay?"

"Oh, yeah, everything is cool," she answered, her tone a little too bubbly in Iris's opinion. *She's up to something, but what?*

"Have you started your homework?"

"Yes, except I have to work on my science project. Aunt Macy is coming over soon to help me with it."

Aunt Macy, Iris thought. When did her sister and Tania get so friendly? After Iris and Macy's little disagreement at the gym, Macy had made a 180-degree turn in her attitude toward Nash. She claimed he didn't seem as bad as the media had made him out to be. It didn't matter now since there was no Iris and Nash.

"Do you need me to pick up any supplies on my way home?"

"No, I'm good. Uncle Nash bought everything I need. Oh, and Ms. Dalton sent over dinner for us. It smells so good, but I'm trying to wait for you before I dive into it."

Iris laughed. In a few weeks when their living arrangement went back to normal, she didn't know who she would miss more Tania, Ms. Dalton…or Nash. It was unlikely Nash would be interested in dating her. Considering his history with women, he probably would have moved on to someone else by then. She wouldn't think about that right now. Besides, before Janna left to return to New York, she had made Iris promise that she would live in the moment and not overthink everything.

"I should be there in about five or ten minutes. I can't wait to see what Ms. D. sent us for dinner."

"Yeah, I can't wait until you see what she sent either," Tania said excitedly.

Once Iris arrived home, instead of going to pick up

her mail first, Iris took the elevator to her penthouse suite. Too exhausted to do more than eat and talk with Tania, she planned to take a shower and be in bed no later than eight o'clock.

The elevator opened and the smell of barbecue teased her senses, making her mouth water the moment she stepped across the threshold.

She kicked the door closed behind her. "Tania, I'm home," she called out and set her jacket and briefcase on the bench next to a tall cobalt-blue floor vase that she'd purchased on a trip to Morocco. "Tania?" she called out again, surprised by the lack of response. After all of the calls from her earlier, Iris was sure she'd be standing by the door.

Iris quickly sifted through the mail that had been left on a stand just inside the entryway, distracted by the amazing aroma from the kitchen. "Mmm, something smells delicious," she said more to herself than to anyone else. She went to place the mail back on the stand, but most of it fell to the floor. *Oh, that's just great.* She bent down to pick it up when a pair of shiny black wing tips appeared out of nowhere. Iris jerked her head up and froze.

"What are you doing here?"

Chapter 10

"Hello to you, too," Nash said when Iris stood and put the mail down. He handed her one of the glasses of white wine that he held. "It's a good thing I don't get offended easily. Otherwise, you could have given me a complex with that greeting."

She nervously ran a hand through her curly locks. "I'm sorry. I'm just…I'm surprised to see you."

"I bet you are, considering you've done your best to avoid me for well over a week." He brought his glass of wine to his lips, staring at her over the rim. After a long day at work, she still looked amazing. Her hair hung loose around her shoulders and the pristine black pantsuit she wore fit every luscious curve of her body as if a tailor had sewn it onto her frame. Nash took a sip of his wine, taking her all in, not caring that he was making her uncomfortable by staring. He had missed her more than he had realized and it was taking Herculean strength not to reach out and pull her into his arms.

She remained silent as she sipped from her glass, looking everywhere but at him. They were standing just inside the foyer and she had yet to try to move past him. *I guess she's doing anything not to risk touching me or me touching her.*

He wanted so badly to pull her into his arms and kiss her sweet lips, but Tania, Macy and Ms. Dalton had gone through a lot of trouble to surprise Iris with dinner. So he needed to stick to the script or deal with their wrath. "We've been set up," he finally said.

"What do you mean?" Iris finally tried to step around him, but he wouldn't move. "Where's Tania?"

"Macy picked her up about twenty minutes ago. They went out to get a few more supplies for Tania's science project, assuming there actually *is* a science project, and then they are heading to Macy's house to work on it."

Iris's hand stilled, the wineglass lingering at her lips. She narrowed her eyes. "Why, that little stinker," she said under her breath, but Nash heard her and smiled.

"You have no idea." He turned to go into the living room, but stopped and looked back. "Dinner is served," he said with a dramatic flourish of his arm. "After you."

Iris slowly followed him into the living room and stopped short. "What in the… How? When?" she said. "This is…amazing."

The illumination from the candles placed strategically around the room, and the dim light hanging from the ceiling above the large flat-screen television, were enough for them to see that Tania and Macy had set up a picnic on the carpet.

Iris picked up the handwritten note sitting on the living room table. "Sit back, relax and enjoy the evening, from the Dynamic Duo." She smirked and placed the note back on the table. "This was very thoughtful."

"Yeah, I was impressed, too, but whoever heard of a carpet picnic?" Nash said, sidling up to Iris, sipping his wine.

She laughed, more relaxed than when she first arrived home. "You are such a guy."

A crooked grin spread across his sexy lips, and Iris suddenly realized that a nice romantic setting probably wasn't the best idea under the circumstances. Her defenses were weak when it came to Nash. He had the movie-star good looks of Shemar Moore and the business savvy of Russell Simmons. Who could control herself when in the presence of a man like that?

"Have a seat on the blanket. I was given strict instructions by Tania and Macy before they left to be at your beck and call…whatever that means." He set his wineglass on the sofa table. "I'll be right back."

Iris had no idea where he was going, but she scurried to her feet and took the opportunity to take a quick glance in the mirror. Had she known he would be there, she would've freshened up before stepping into the apartment. Seeing that her makeup was fine, she slipped out of her suit jacket and tossed it on the sofa, which had been moved to the perimeter of the room. "All right, here we go." Nash returned from the kitchen with steaming hot barbecue ribs on a platter.

He sat them on a tray on top of the blanket and grabbed the picnic basket from the coffee table.

"Are you sure you didn't know anything about this carpet picnic?"

"Hell, I never even heard of a carpet picnic."

"What? That means you've never seen *Pretty Woman.* How could that be?" she said, feigning shock.

Nash turned to her and furrowed his brows. "Isn't it a chick flick?"

"Yeah, but surely you've seen a chick flick before."

"If nothing's being blown up or no heads are rolling down an alley, I'm not interested." He unloaded the rest of the large picnic basket and handed the dishes to Iris, who placed them in the center of the blanket. When he pulled out the last item, he let out a loud groan.

Iris fell over laughing. Ms. Dalton and the girls had thought of everything. She reached for the *Pretty Woman* DVD dangling from Nash's fingers and held it to her chest.

"This is my all-time favorite movie. I'm going to have to kiss Ms. Dalton the next time I see her."

"In the meantime, you can always kiss me." Nash grabbed the movie from her hand and tossed it to the side. He skirted around the food and crawled up to her, forcing her to lie back on the blanket. "I've missed you," he said against her lips, his body hovering over hers.

Iris, her hands resting on his biceps, reveled in the feel of his taut muscles against her palms and his large frame perched above her. "I've missed you, too."

As he coaxed her lips apart, the gentle massage of his tongue and the taste of his delicious mouth sent currents of desire roaring through her body. Considering how hungry she had been when she first walked in, food suddenly wasn't the main thing on her mind. For the first time in weeks, she didn't care what Noelle said; she wanted Nash more than any man she'd ever known. Not a day had gone by that she hadn't thought of him and dreamed of the next time she would be in his arms. His hand moved slowly up and down her body. She felt transported on a soft and delicate cloud as he pulled her closer and his mouth teased hers, offering a pledge of greater things to come.

How could she tell him that she wanted more than just his kisses without sounding loose? All the tantalizing actions he was doing were driving her nuts. Her thoughts became jumbled when he placed kisses along her cheek, searing a path down to her neck, while his hand roamed along the side of her body. When he worked his way back up and stopped to nibble at her earlobe, sending goose bumps up and down her arms, she felt she would jump out of her skin at any moment if he didn't stop the sweet torture.

"Nash," she breathed between parted lips. "I…I—"

"You've missed me, missed my touch," he said against her neck, unbuttoning her shirt and easing it open.

A knot rose in her throat as his large hand cupped her breast. His skilled fingers tweaked her hardened nipple through the thin material of her lace bra.

"Right now, I don't care why you've been avoiding me. Just take me to your bedroom, so I can show you how much I've missed you." He raised his head and unsnapped the front of her bra, his desire-laden gaze fixed on her. "This time when I make you come, I want you on a soft surface…and naked. I plan to worship this gorgeous body of yours until the sun comes up."

Iris swallowed hard. She was no longer shocked by her body's eager response to Nash's mouth on her skin, but the thought of making love to him had every nerve ending within her going crazy.

He lowered his head and captured a nipple between his teeth, his tongue rotating and teasing mercilessly, causing her to squirm beneath him, her throbbing sex ready for anything he had in mind.

"Nash," she cried, her eyes shut tight as she feverishly grasped at the back of his shirt in an effort to catch her breath. She wanted more, but she didn't think her heart could take much more of the erotic pleasure pumping through her veins. When he repeated the action on the other nipple, she knew it was only a matter of minutes before she reached that point of no return.

"Nash," she panted, shouting his name again. "Okay, okay, let's go upstairs…please."

With one last delectable swirl of his tongue, he sat back and took in her body, still caressing her breast.

"Nash."

"All right, but you stopped me just in time." Her eyes closed at his touch. *God, if he can make me feel this good and he's only gotten as far as my breasts, I might not be able to handle much more.*

"Let's go," he said, his voice hoarse and sexy.

He helped her up and then made quick work of blowing out the candles before he followed her upstairs to her bedroom. Within minutes, he had them out of their clothes and Iris's heart thundered and her knees went weak at the sight of the well-built Adonis standing before her. Broad shoulders and a chiseled chest caught her attention first, but as her gaze traveled beyond his narrow waist and washboard abs, her only thought was that he was utter perfection. God had truly done his best work when he created this man.

Iris didn't know how long she stood marveling at him. All she wanted to do was touch him everywhere, to feel his hard, sinewy muscles contract against her hands. She glanced up to find Nash gawking at her and she didn't know what aroused her more—looking at him in all of his glory, or watching the way he perused her nude body.

"I knew you would be beautiful, but you're absolutely exquisite," he said just above a whisper.

I was just thinking the same thing about you. Always self-conscious about her body and height, this was the first time that she could remember not feeling insecure about the color of her skin, her naturally curly hair or her too-long legs. The way Nash's eyes raked over her, assessing every inch of her body, made her feel as if she was the most desirable woman he'd ever seen.

He backed her to the bed and she sat on the king-size mattress, acutely aware that she had a naked man, and not just anyone, but *Nash Dupree,* in her bedroom.

"I have wanted you from the moment I laid eyes on you and I intend to have you…all of you."

He grabbed a couple of condoms from his wallet and placed them on the nightstand before he climbed onto the bed and lay beside her. His hand gently outlined the circle of her breast and her eyes fluttered closed. It was as if he knew just the right things to do. His touch was light and painfully teasing, so much so that her body tingled with a passion she'd never experienced before.

For weeks, she'd wondered what it would be like to be intimate with him, and tonight, that would be a reality.

She placed her hand on his hard chest, loving the feel of the soft hairs sifting through her fingers. It all seemed surreal. How many times had she seen him in magazines, his handsome face smiling back at her, leaving her to wonder what type of person he was. Now here he was, in her life, in her house and in her bed.

She lay in the crook of Nash's arm, making circular motions on his chest and toying with his flat nipples. Lost in the pleasure of how good he felt, she suddenly shivered when he ran his hand along the side of her body, sending electric shock waves to every nerve ending. Considering how much of a hurry he was in to get her into bed, she wondered why he wasn't doing even more to get things started. No sooner had she had that last thought than he gently covered her hand on his chest with his. She gazed into his sexy hazel eyes.

Without a word, he steered her hand down over his flat abs, lingering for a moment, before he guided her to his engorged shaft. Iris sucked in a breath, awed by how huge he felt in her hands. She would have never been bold enough to make such a move, but now her hand had a mind of its own.

She stroked the length of him, reveling in the warm smoothness of his skin and shuddering at the feel of him growing enticingly hard in her palm. She gripped him tighter, unable to help herself, and his eyes slammed shut as a result. A deep groan slipped through his lips when she massaged and fondled the tip of him with the pad of her thumb. Moisture pooled between her thighs and butterflies erupted in her gut as Nash started moving against her hand, forcing her hand to slide up and down his shaft rhythmically.

Iris felt empowered knowing that she could bring him pleasure with just a touch here and a squeeze there. She moved her hand on his length, increasing and decreasing the tension and the speed, amazed at how stimulated he was getting with every glide of her hand. Nash uttered a sharp moan and he jerked out of her grip, cursing under his breath as he pushed her flat onto her back. His strong body covered hers and he had her arms pinned above her head. The bondage-like move made her recall their rendezvous in the gym weeks ago, and she liked the position even more now than she had then.

"If I had let you continue touching me the way you were," he said, his voice deep and intoxicating, "this would've been over before we got started good."

With one hand, he maintained a loose grip on her arms. As he lowered his mouth to hers, his free hand roamed over her body, exploring every inch. She breathed into his mouth and wiggled beneath his scorching touch, her body on fire.

The prolonged anticipation of their union was almost unbearable as he took his time on her body. "Ah, Nash," she whimpered when his tongue connected with one of her swollen nipples and his hand eased between her thighs. She bit down on her bottom lip, trying to hold it together, as one finger, and then another, entered her throbbing sex. Iris felt her mind leave her body, and she couldn't ever remember feeling the kind of erotic force that now churned inside her body.

Her breath came in short spurts as a volcanic quake brewed within her and she moved frantically against his hand. His fingers dipped, swirled and teased, stirring the passion threatening to explode. "I don't think…I can hold on."

Nash released her arms, but he didn't stop the excruciating torture between her thighs. Instead, he increased the speed, going deeper and harder, faster and rougher. A scream lodged in her throat and she grabbed a handful of the satin sheet in her fist, tremors of pleasure causing her to teeter on the edge.

"Go ahead, sweetheart. Let's get this first one out of the way," he crooned, kneeling over her and not letting up the sweet torment to her body. "We have all night."

Within seconds, she screamed her release. "Oh, my God…*Nash!*" she cried, her body bucking against his fingers, her head thrashing back and forth against the pillow. She clawed at his arms, shoulders and chest, unable to get a grip on him or catch her breath. It was if she were submerged underwater, panting and fighting her way through the deep, unable to make it to the surface.

Tears burned the back of her eyes when finally Nash's face came into focus. *Never have I ever experienced anything so intensely sensational in all of my life.*

Not waiting for Iris to recover, Nash eased between her legs, his knees nudging her thighs apart. Witnessing her explosive orgasm only fueled the embers burning within him, and he yearned to be inside her. Frenzied need pumped wildly through his veins as he made quick work of covering his shaft. He perched above her, his hands on each side of her head. He searched her eyes for a sign that she was ready for him.

"Nash," she whimpered, as if reading his mind.

The emotion he saw in her eyes was almost his undoing. She put her hands on his waist, guiding him to give her what she wanted, which was all the encouragement he needed. He lingered around her opening, his erection bumping against her slick entrance before he eased inside her, taking it as slowly as humanly possible, allowing her body to adjust to him. Hot and unbelievably tight, she wrapped around him like a new leather glove, snug and warm.

Nash wanted to take his time and love her the way she deserved to be loved, but she felt so good. He captured one perky nipple between his teeth and sucked greedily, his tongue swirling around it thoroughly before giving the other one the same honor.

She wrapped her long legs around him, fusing their bodies together. Nash sucked in a breath, trying to slow his erratic heartbeat, when her hands gripped his butt and pulled him closer. He didn't think he could maintain the slow, erotic rhythm he had started, especially with the way she moved beneath him. He willed his body to stay in control, but the deeper he buried himself in her, the more out of control he felt. *To hell with it.*

He increased his pace, slamming into her faster and faster, their bodies rubbing against each other with each powerful thrust. She matched his moves stroke for stroke, pulling him in deeper and deeper, the strength of her legs rocking him in and out of her.

"Nash," she hoarsely cried, her inner walls pulsating around him, gripping him tightly. She screamed out again and dug her nails into his shoulders, her body twitching and jerking uncontrollably with the reverberations of her orgasm. "Yes, yes…ah, yes!"

Nash knew he would never get tired of her screaming his name. When he heard it, he felt like a car being jump-started. Not giving her the chance to come down off her high, he gripped her hips, raising her slightly off the bed, and thrust into her womanly folds, deeper and harder, as she clung to his shoulders, moaning with every thrust. Her legs tightened around his waist as the turbulence of her passion swirled around him.

He could no longer maintain a grip on his control. He bucked and jerked wildly against her; his heart slammed into his chest and heat spread through his body as the intensity of his release spun him out of control. "Iris!" he growled between clenched teeth. The involuntary tremors of ecstasy shook him to the core and a guttural howl ripped through his lips, overpowering all other sounds in the room.

Sated and out of breath, he collapsed against her, careful to bear most of his weight as he struggled onto his back. An aftershock of their lovemaking then rocked him to the central part of his being and he shuddered, pulling Iris tightly into his arms.

He lay panting next to her, their chests heaving against each other, delighting in the aftermath of the most amazing sex he'd ever had. Never had he ever felt a connection, both mentally and physically, with anyone the way he did with Iris at that very moment.

As her breathing slowed, she threw her arm across his waist and snuggled closer, his chin resting upon her head. Nash held her against his body, sighing with pleasant exhaustion, as his eyes drifted closed.

Chapter 11

Hours later, candlelight flickered in the cozy bathroom, soft jazz flowing through the overhead speaker. Iris sighed with contentment as she leaned against Nash, enjoying their romantic bubble bath. She sat between his legs, bubbles up to her chest, her head resting against his shoulder, loving the feel of his body behind her.

After eating in bed, they had made love again, then dozed off. She didn't think she would ever get enough of him. His skilled hands and lips, and the way he worshipped her body, had given a whole new meaning to rocking her world.

"I love that you're a screamer," Nash said out of nowhere. Iris swallowed hard and stiffened in his arms. "I didn't say that to embarrass you. I like that your body responds to me with so much passion and that I'm able to make you scream."

"I didn't know I was a screamer," she said quietly, not sure how else to respond. "It's never happened with anyone. I have never felt…" she started, but stopped, deciding that she didn't have to tell him about her pitiful sex life. "I won't ever forget tonight."

"Me, either."

Neither of them spoke again until Iris said, "I'm going to have to do something very special for Ms. D., Tania and Macy," she said as Nash nuzzled the side of her neck. He dragged the sponge from the water and raked it across her chest and around her neck.

"Yeah, me, too."

She closed her eyes and moaned when he took the sponge lower, making circular motions near her most intimate area. "You know, a girl could get used to a handsome man like yourself bathing her and showering her with all of this attention."

"Is that right?" Iris could hear the humor in his voice and loved how comfortable he made her feel.

"Yep. Maybe I can hire you a couple of times a week to be at my beck and call."

"Sweetheart, you don't have to hire me. I'll always make myself available to you. And since we're on the subject, let's talk about your reason for avoiding me lately."

Iris sighed, not wanting to ruin the moment with this conversation. Noelle's words had crept into her mind a couple of times during the evening, but she'd been able to push them back and focus on the here and now.

"Nash, we've already talked about this. It's not a good idea for you and me to date right now."

Except for the rain hitting the windowpane, silence suddenly filled the dimly lit space.

"How can you make a decision to stop seeing me based on some stupid photo? I actually liked the picture. It captured the fun we were having that evening and it showed how much we enjoy each other's company."

Nash pulled her closer against him, her butt rubbing against his groin, making it hard for her to think. She couldn't believe she was actually taking a bath with a man. The fact that the man happened to be *Nash Dupree,* who was arguing his reasons for wanting to date her, made it feel more like a dream than reality.

"Iris, I don't give a damn about the tabloids. There will always be paparazzi lurking around, butting into my business...*our* business...but I don't care about all of that. All I want is to be with you."

He lifted her hair from her shoulders and placed a kiss on the side of her neck. "The paparazzi don't rule my life. I have always marched my own beat and there is no way I'm going to let some pests come between us." He turned her slightly so she could look at him. "Are you concerned what people will think of you hanging out with me?"

"Yes," she said simply and turned fully in his arms and onto her knees, her hands resting against his chest. "Nash, technically you're going through a custody battle. It might not seem that way, but that's exactly what it is. Until you prove to the courts that you're a fit parent, they will not allow Tania to return home."

His gaze zoned in on her bare breasts and he pulled her closer until she was flat against his chest. Nipping at her ear, he groaned. "I can't think straight with your naked body tempting me like this."

Iris's eyes drifted shut. Her moans filled the space

as his hands caressed her bottom and slowly worked their way up her spine. When her arms eased around his neck, she caught herself.

"Wait. Stop." She pulled back and folded her arms across her chest, obstructing his view of her breasts. "You're the one who started this conversation, so let's finish it."

Nash closed his eyes and rested his head against the tiled wall. Iris took that opportunity to climb out of the bathtub and grab one of the thick towels that she had laid out for them.

"Iris, I've done everything I've been assigned to do." He lifted his head and met her gaze, not bothering to move from his position in the bathtub. "I have relinquished Tania into your care, gone through the individual counseling sessions, and Tania and I will be starting family counseling in the next couple of weeks. All of this to prove to some judge, who thinks of me as an unfit parent, that I've been a better father to Tania than some fathers are to their biological children."

"Honey, I know it doesn't sound fair, but unfortunately you have to prove it. The judge based his decision on the information he had—Tania's recent trouble with the law, the issues she was having at school and the not-so-favorable photos of you in the tabloids. You being seen socializing with me, a person who is technically your child's guardian, might not look good to the public. And you know reporters are great at twisting the truth of a story in order to sell more copies of their trashy magazines."

He rose from the bathtub and Iris's breath hitched in her throat. His well-toned body, glistening with water dripping from every muscle, was doing wicked things to her. It took everything she had to stay put and keep her hands to herself.

Iris grabbed the towel and handed it to him. She watched as he haphazardly dried himself, not taking his gaze from her. He stepped out of the tub and, instead of wrapping the towel around himself, he dropped it to the floor and approached her.

"I can't even begin to tell you how much you mean to me." His long arms snaked around her waist. "I know it's only been a short time, but I feel a connection to you that I have *never* felt for any other woman in my life."

"Nash." She placed her soft palm against the light stubble on his cheek, trying to ignore the fact that his naked body was rubbing up against her. "I feel the same about you, but you're a celebrity in Atlanta. Just because you don't want the outside world all up in your business, doesn't mean that's how it's going to be."

"No one knows about this custody thing with Tania or the trouble she's gotten herself into."

"Not yet, but you know how resourceful these reporters are. How many times have you been in the tabloids over the past six months?" When he didn't respond, she continued, "Enough times for you to know that if they want to find something out, they will."

Days later, Iris walked into her apartment to the smell of Pine-Sol and Pledge furniture polish. "I'm home," she called out. She decided to carry her briefcase and purse to her bedroom instead of leaving the items near the door as she usually did. Tania had called earlier, asking if she could invite some friends over, and Iris didn't want to clutter the apartment.

"Hey, Iris," Tania said when Iris stopped by the kitchen before heading upstairs.

"Sorry, I'm a little late. Glad to see that I beat your friends here."

"They probably won't get here for another half an hour. Lauren is picking everyone up and she's always late." Tania poured herself a glass of lemonade. "Want some?" She held up the pitcher.

"Sure." Iris placed her items in one of the chairs at the small kitchen table and took a seat at the breakfast bar.

She didn't know how she was going to be able to return to a normal life after Tania left. Having someone to come home to reminded her of just how empty her life had been. Until recently, her career had been her top priority, but Tania and Nash had her thinking more and more about having a family of her own.

"So, who's all coming over?" Iris sipped from her lemonade and squinted, wondering how Tania could stand the drink to be so sweet.

"Lauren, Sarah and Megan." Tania said, standing on other side of the bar.

Iris nodded. "Do you remember the first day we met and you said someone planted those drugs on you?" They hadn't talked much about the marijuana found on Tania, but it was never far from her mind, especially since Tania was determined to find the person who set her up.

Tania nodded.

"Do you think it was one of the girls you're inviting over?"

Tania stared down into her glass of lemonade, running her finger around the top of the vessel. "Maybe."

Iris knew Tania was too smart to be completely clueless about who might have planted those drugs on her. Though Noelle had met with the parents of the students who were in the car with Tania, so far, no one had come forward about the drugs.

"Well, we've never talked about this, but there are a few things I do not allow." Iris stood and added some water to her glass of lemonade before returning to her seat. "There's no alcohol, drugs or foul language allowed here. I expect your friends to treat *our* home the way you and I treat it. Do you understand?"

Tania nodded. "Yes."

"I'll hang out upstairs while they're here, so you guys can have your space. If you see someone doing something they shouldn't be doing, or they are not following the rules, come and find me. Okay?"

"Okay." Tania walked around the counter and over to Iris. "I really appreciate everything you've done for me...and I just want you to know that if my mother was alive, I'd want her to be just like you."

Within seconds, tears filled Iris's eyes. "Oh, baby," she said, pulling Tania into her arms. She placed a kiss against her cheek. "If I had a daughter, I'd want her to be just like you. I love you, sweetie."

"Love you, too."

They were both wiping their eyes when the telephone rang.

"I'll let you get that. It might be Rob calling to let you know your friends are downstairs."

"It's them," Tania said when she hung up the phone. "They're on their way up."

"Okay. I'm going to run my things upstairs, but I'll be down shortly to meet them."

Minutes later when Iris walked back downstairs, she was greeted with lots of laughing and loud talking. It brought back fond memories of when she, Janna and Macy were kids. How many times had Mama Adel threatened to put them out of the house if they didn't tone it down?

"Hi, girls," Iris said when she walked into the kitchen, where they all were grabbing snacks and drinks.

"Hi," they chorused.

"This is Iris. She's my uncle's girlfriend," Tania said without missing a beat.

Iris stood, dumbfounded, staring at Tania. She hadn't officially named her role in Nash's life, but if she had to be honest, Iris liked the idea of being his woman. Considering the amount of time they'd been spending together, and the fact that she had been his date to a few events, Iris could see where Tania would get that idea.

A few hours passed. Iris had tried getting work done while the girls were watching their movie, but she couldn't concentrate. She hadn't dated often, and could only remember one relationship that had the potential of leading to the possibility of marriage. The idea of being Nash's woman swam around in her head, but could she really handle being his girlfriend? His lifestyle? The women? Rarely did they go anyplace where he wasn't recognized or approached by some bold woman.

"I think I'm going to go to bed," Tania said, interrupting Iris's thoughts.

"All right, have a good night. Uh, Tania?" Iris said, catching her before she walked out of the kitchen and up the stairs.

"Yes."

"What made you tell your friends that your uncle and I were dating?"

Tania hesitated and then said, "Ms. D. always says that if you want something to happen in your life, claim it and have faith that it will happen." Tania shrugged. "So I did. See you in the morning."

For the second time that night, Iris was left speechless. The thought of having Tania—and Nash—in her life forever felt like too much to hope for. After all, no one got everything they wished for, and that kind of happily-ever-after was just too much to hope for.

Chapter 12

Iris scanned the dimly lit room from the table where she sat with Macy in the VIP section of Platinum Pieces–Midtown. She had seen the new club, but tonight, to celebrate her birthday, Nash had invited her to his swanky Midtown Atlanta location. The mellow sounds coming from the band that graced the stage, the chatter from the crowd that was growing by the second and the intimacy of the space reminded her of a blues-and-jazz club she visited during a trip to New Orleans.

Unlike the new location, this space had a juke-joint feel. An antique jukebox on display near the bar held a couple of people's attention, while a few others grooved on the dance floor to the smooth tunes of the house band. Iris bobbed her head to the beat as she continued to glance around, noticing for the first time that some of the walls were made of exposed red brick and decorated with artwork with figures from the history of jazz. The industrial-like ceiling and painted concrete floor brought everything together beautifully. Whoever had done the decor had done a fine job. The establishment was the perfect spot to kick back and unwind after a hectic week.

From Iris's vantage point at the side of the stage, she could see most of the people in the club, including Nash. He had shown her and Macy to their table earlier, but had since been working the room, greeting, shaking hands and allowing kisses on the cheek from more than one woman.

"I know what you're thinking," Macy whispered near Iris's ear. "He's working. Just because women are all up in his face doesn't mean he's interested."

Iris glanced at her. "What are you, a mind reader or something?"

Macy laughed. "No, but when it comes to Nash, you wear your feelings on your face like a glaring neon sign reading *off-limits* in bright green letters. You might want to start using the game face you use when going head-to-head with opposing counsel, because the jealous, insecure frown you're exhibiting now is not very becoming."

Iris turned back to where Nash stood now talking with yet another woman. Macy was right, but Iris couldn't help it. She and Nash had only been seeing each other for a short while, but her insecurities reared their wicked heads from time to time. He was *the* Nash Dupree: multimillionaire, Atlanta's most eligible bachelor and a notorious playboy according to the media.

As if sensing her eyes on him, Nash glanced at her. Iris's pulse quickened when he winked. The sexy grin on his face was one he flashed often, which made her palms sweaty and her panties wet. Her gaze followed him across the room and onto the stage, where he accepted the mic from the lead singer. Just the sight of him, standing there in his dark gray double-breasted suit, sent her pulse running wild.

Nash tapped the mic to get everyone's attention. "Good evening, all," he said in that deep, sexy voice that still made Iris's heart beat double time. "Thank you for coming out to Platinum Pieces and celebrating with us tonight. I have a birthday surprise for a very special lady tonight, so you picked a good evening to join us for some live entertainment. A very dear friend and world-renowned performer is here to celebrate with us. Please join me in welcoming R&B/neo-soul singer-songwriter Mikale."

Iris's mouth fell open. *Oh, my God! Nash is friends with Mikale?* He was only her all-time favorite R&B singer, one she had a major crush on. She had all of his CDs and had seen him perform on more than one occasion.

"Your man's coming this way," Macy whispered. "And whatever you do, please don't overthink tonight. Just go with *whatever* he proposes."

The band started playing the first few notes of "My Life with You," and Nash weaved his way through the crowd until he stood before her. "I understand that this is one of your favorites. Would you do me the honor of dancing with me?"

"Nash…" How did he know this was her favorite song?

"Just one dance."

"Well, if she won't dance with you, suga, I will,"

a woman from the table next to Iris's, who looked to be in her mid-fifties, leaned over and said. "I'd never pass up an opportunity to dance with a hunk like you."

Nash smiled at the woman and then turned back to Iris with a pleading look in his eyes. "Please," he mouthed silently.

Iris laughed and pushed away from the table, accepting his hand and allowing him to guide her to the semicrowded dance floor.

"Happy birthday, baby," Nash said and pulled her against his hard body. She was conscious of where his hands landed on her lower back, just above her butt. His touch sent a delicious shiver through her body.

"Thank you. This was very thoughtful," she said close to his ear.

Iris had missed being in his arms. With Tania in her house, they tried to be on their best behavior, except for the time when Nash cornered her in the bathroom for a quickie. Tania knew they saw each other on occasion, but Iris didn't want Tania to think of her as one of those women who allowed a man to stay overnight when their kids were in the house.

She snuggled closer, her arms around Nash's neck, loving how good and relaxed he made her feel. When he rested his cheek against hers, turning slightly and placing a tender kiss on the side of her face, she inhaled his fresh, clean scent and snuggled closer.

"Did I tell you how beautiful you look tonight?"

Iris smiled. "You might have mentioned it once or twice." She had worn a short black dress Janna had sent her a couple of weeks ago.

Nash's breath caressed the sensitive spot behind Iris's ear as he held her securely against his hard body;

Iris thought she would melt. The tenderness of his lips against her blazing skin was almost unbearable. A simple little kiss had her fantasizing about other areas she'd like for him to touch and remembering the night of their carpet picnic. Her heart raced at the memory.

"May I cut in?"

Iris's eyes flew open. A fair-skinned woman with long auburn hair and light brown eyes stood before her. She looked vaguely familiar, but Iris couldn't remember where she'd seen her before.

"Do you mind?" she asked Iris, a small smile across her lips that didn't reach her eyes.

"Even if she doesn't, I do," Nash growled in a low, barely controlled voice. "What are you doing here, Eve?"

Iris glanced at Nash, surprised by the tightening of his jaw and the lethal glint in his narrowed eyes. Before the woman could say anything, Ace, Nash's bouncer-turned-bodyguard, appeared out of nowhere. Over the past couple of weeks, Nash had received several calls that he had assumed were pranks. It wasn't until a threatening note showed up two days ago that he started taking the situation seriously. When the police admitted to not being able to pull any prints from the note, Nigel had insisted that Nash needed a bodyguard. The fact that the paparazzi had been showing up at the oddest times helped in the decision.

"Please show Ms. Vanlough out," Nash instructed Ace.

"I'm not going away, Nash!" the woman seethed, ignoring the curious stares from nearby patrons and the fact that Ace was practically carrying her to the front entrance.

Iris remembered her now. She was an actress who had appeared in a couple of movies a few years back and had recently landed a role on a television series. Iris would think that Eve would be concerned about her public behavior, but apparently not.

Nash pulled Iris back into his arms and returned to dancing as if nothing had happened.

"Care to explain?"

"That was Eve Vanlough. She and I dated for a while, but we broke up earlier this year."

When he didn't elaborate, Iris asked, "Does she know?"

"Does she know what?"

"That you guys have broken up. It looked as though she was still very much interested in you."

Nash slowed his steps and leaned back to look at her, still keeping pace with the slow song. "She knows. But so that *you* know, there is nothing—and I mean absolutely *nothing*—between her and me." He placed a kiss on Iris's temple and pulled her closer to him. "You're the only woman I'm interested in."

Is this what she had to look forward to when spending time in public with Nash? Before her conversation with Noelle weeks ago, she had experienced women flirting with Nash and giving him second looks, but since he didn't seem to pay it any mind, she hadn't either. But this was different. This woman was someone he had actually admitted to dating. A woman who clearly wasn't ready to let him go.

She wrapped her arms tighter around Nash's neck, hoping that he was telling her the truth and that he and Eve were over.

"Come to my office with me," Nash whispered, his breath warm against her ear.

At that moment, the way his voice made her body tingle, Iris would have gone to the moon with him.

She glanced at the stage, where Mikale had transitioned into his next song, continuing to sing as if Eve hadn't just interrupted his set. Iris returned her gaze to Nash.

"What about the rest of the show? I don't know when I'll get to hear Mikale live again, especially from this vantage point."

Nash placed a light kiss on her lips. "I promise you, sweetheart, this will not be the last time you see him perform. You have my word. Come with me." He stepped back and tugged on her hand.

She smiled at him and without a word they walked hand in hand toward his office She didn't know what he had planned in his office, but if it gave her an opportunity to taste his sweet lips, she was all for it.

Nash unlocked his office door and directed Iris into the large, dimly lit room, locking the door behind them.

"So, what did you want to talk about?" Iris asked softly, her heart thumping loudly in her ears. She stood across the room from him and anxiety pulsed through her veins at the raw longing that gleamed in his intense hazel eyes. Suddenly she didn't think talking was what he had in mind.

He stared at her without speaking. His gaze traveled slowly down the length of her body and she fidgeted under the intensity of his stare, tugging on her tight-fitted off-the-shoulder dress. Suddenly, self-conscious of her hardened nipples pushing against the thin fabric, she folded her arms across her chest. She was being ridiculous, but he was making her hot all over.

"Nash..." she breathed just as he took two long strides and pulled her against the solid length of his hard body.

"I want you so bad I ache." He ravaged her lips and made quick work of sliding her dress off her shoulders, and worked it all the way down her legs, barely taking his lips from hers. He finally let her up for air and helped her step out of the flimsy garment.

She stood before him in her black strapless bra, barely-there matching panties, thigh-high nylons and black stilettos. His gaze raked over her hungrily and Iris's insides melted like a stick of butter sitting on a windowsill during a hot summer day.

By the way he hurried out of his clothes, it was clear that they weren't going to spend the rest of the evening talking.

"Damn, woman!" Nash said huskily. Lying on the oversize sofa in his office, he rolled off Iris and onto his back. He pulled her into the crook of his arm and yanked the light throw from the back of the sofa down over them. "I think you're trying to kill me."

"I could say the same for you." Iris swung her arm across his waist, her rapid heartbeat pounding against his chest. "You were like a madman. What's gotten into you? I could barely keep up."

Nash chuckled. "I'm sorry, sweetheart. Dancing with you had me all excited, but seeing you in your sexy underwear—" he shrugged "—I just couldn't control myself."

Never had he met a woman who fulfilled his intellectual and sexual appetite the way Iris did. They had only had sex once since the night that Tania and Macy set them up, and that was a quickie in the bathroom. Nash thought he would explode when he first saw her enter the club in her sexy outfit. It didn't help matters that a few other men were checking her out. Nash had been quick to get to her and remove all doubt that she was there alone. As soon as she'd entered, he'd planted a kiss on her that had a few nearby patrons whistling and telling them to get a room. He had thought for sure that Iris would give him a hard time about the public display of affection, but instead she had ducked her head and tried to hide a smile.

"I'll be right back," Nash said and kissed Iris on her forehead before making his way to the en-suite bathroom. When he returned, he climbed back under the blanket and pulled her back into his arms. In the distance he could hear the band playing one of his favorite songs.

"What are you thinking about?" Iris asked, cutting into his thoughts.

"Not too much, but there is something I wanted to talk to you about." Iris stiffened in his arms. "Relax, baby, it's not bad."

"Then what is it?" She lifted up and Nash met her gaze.

"I want to talk about us."

"What about us?"

"Though I haven't been with anyone since meeting you, I was wondering how you felt about us being exclusive."

She hesitated before speaking. "Are you sure that's what you want? What about Eve?"

"Iris, Eve is a nonissue. And to answer your other question, yes, it's what I want. I have never felt for another woman what I feel for you. The more I'm with you, the more I want to be with you, but I need to know if you feel the same way."

Iris nodded. "I do. Nash, these past couple of months with you have been wonderful, and I'd like to see where this could go. Now that doesn't mean that I'm not concerned about us being seen in public right now, and don't get me started about that kiss you laid on me earlier."

Nash grinned. He knew she would bring that kiss up at some point. "So, Counselor, does this mean that we're a couple?"

Iris laughed. "Oh, I guess," she said, feigning disinterest.

Nash wrapped both arms around her and pulled her on top of him. "I'm thinking maybe we should seal this agreement with a little *somethin'-somethin'*."

"Ooh, I like the way you think, Mr. Dupree."

A loud knock at the door caused Iris to jump and pull herself out of Nash's arms. She made a move to climb over him, no doubt to hurry and get dressed, but Nash stopped her. "Whoever it is, I'll get rid of them." He slid into his pants, not bothering with his shirt or socks. Only a few people had access to the hallway that led to his office.

The persistent person knocked again and Nash hurried to the door, wanting to pummel whoever had ruined the moment.

"What?" He swung the door open ready to launch harsher words at the intruder. At first no one was there, but then Nigel stepped in front of the doorway.

"We have a situa…" he started, but stopped after a quick glance at Nash. "Uh…never mind. I'm sure I can handle it." He turned on his heels and hurried away.

Nash grinned and shook his head before he closed and locked the door.

"So, where were we?"

Chapter 13

Iris pulled three evening gowns from her closet and laid them across the bed as she mulled over which one to wear. The night of her birthday, over two weeks ago, Nash had asked her to attend a fund-raiser with him as his date. Despite Noelle's warning about them being seen together while Nash was dealing with his custody issues, Iris had accepted.

"Where do you see yours and Nash's relationship going?" Macy asked. She stood next to Iris, examining the evening gowns.

"I'm taking one day at a time," Iris said. "Of course I would love to get married and have a family one day, but I don't want to jinx this. I want our relationship to naturally progress and if it leads to marriage, wonderful, and if not—" she shrugged "—I'll look at it as an awesome experience."

Who was she kidding? If things didn't work out between her and Nash, she would be crushed. He was the first man to ever make her feel special, make her feel desirable.

"I'm sure Nash was as surprised as I was that you agreed to be his date for that upcoming Holding It Together annual fund-raiser. I attended it a couple of years ago and it's a huge deal. A lot of movers and shakers will be there and this event is usually widely publicized. Are you ready to see another photo of you and Nash in a magazine or in one of the local newspapers?"

Iris hadn't thought of that, but she didn't want to keep saying no to Nash regarding public appearances, especially one that supported single parents of children with leukemia. Last week she saw him in a photo with an actress who starred in Tyler Perry's last movie and her heart dropped. Nash had explained that he and the woman had done a commercial together earlier that year and were friends. But that didn't stop the tabloid from speculating that he was involved with the pretty actress.

"I'm not sure I'm ready. I still question whether or not it's a good idea to put our relationship on display, but I want these little hussies to know he's off the market."

Macy's eyebrows shot up and she jumped off the love seat. She pumped her fist in the air. "Go ahead, sis, claim your man! Let those little gold-diggers know what's up."

They both burst out laughing. Iris didn't know what she would do without her sisters. Since the death of her mother, Janna and Macy had been her rocks, and it didn't matter that they weren't biologically related;

the bonds they shared were ones she would treasure until her dying day.

They collapsed on the love seat. "I know I initially gave you a hard time about Nash, but I have to admit, I like him. He's definitely not like I thought he would be; granted, all I had to go on was what I saw in those trash mags, but I can honestly say I think he's a great catch."

Iris leaned over and bumped shoulders with Macy. "It means a lot to hear you say that. I like him, too…a lot. As a matter of fact, I think I'm in love with him, and it scares the heck out of me. What if he doesn't feel the same way?"

"Oh, please. I've seen the way Nash looks at you and how he treats you and I have to admit, I think he's falling hard."

Iris grabbed hold of her sister's arm and grinned. "You really think so?"

"Girl, yes." She stood and pulled Iris up with her. "Now, let's get serious. We need to decide which of these gowns is going to knock the socks off your man tomorrow night."

Nash stood at the bar nursing his second scotch, wondering what was taking Iris so long. This was the night of the Holding It Together fund-raiser. Two weeks ago, when he'd asked Iris to be his date for the event, he thought for sure she would decline and tell him they needed to keep their relationship quiet awhile longer. She'd shocked him by agreeing to attend, but called him a couple of hours ago and said that she would have to meet him and Tania there. One of her clients who was on probation had gotten into some trouble.

Nash sauntered across the crowded ballroom of the

Marriott Marquis toward his table. Dupree Enterprises was one of the major contributors for the event, sponsoring a table of eight for $4,000. As far as Nash was concerned, it was well worth it. Holding It Together had a good reputation of supporting its families. Now if only he could get his bad attitude together, maybe he could actually enjoy the evening.

For the past couple of weeks, Iris had been the first thing he thought about when he woke up and the last thing he thought about when his head hit the pillow. It was freaking him out. Never had he ever felt so strongly for a woman, wanting to spend every waking hour with her. He was having a hard time adjusting to the unfamiliar need to know where she was and what she was doing at all times.

"She'll be here, Uncle Nash," Tania whispered in his ear when he reclaimed his seat. It amazed him how intuitive she was. "And wait until you see her dress. It's going to blow your mind." She grinned.

Yeah, that's all I need. Iris in a sexy dress with other men gawking at her all night. When had he become the jealous and possessive type? It was Iris. She was everything he wanted and needed in a woman, and it scared the hell out of him.

As if his mind had conjured her up, Iris walked in and his stomach bottomed out. Breathtaking wasn't a strong enough description to describe how she looked tonight. He didn't understand how she could get more beautiful each time he saw her. She was an absolute knockout in a red, strapless ball gown with sparkling gems on the bodice of the dress; her hair was piled on top of her head with a few curly tendrils hanging in her face.

"Close your mouth, man. Something might fly in," Nigel teased when he walked back to the table carrying two glasses of wine, one for him and one for his wife.

"I told you her dress was going to blow your mind," Tania whispered again. "Doesn't she look hot?"

Not trusting himself to speak, Nash could only nod. He noticed Iris glancing around the large ballroom, looking for them. A small smile tilted her lips when she spotted him, and all the blood in his heart rushed to his groin when their eyes connected.

He blew out a ragged breath. This woman did wicked things to him and he didn't know if he would ever get used to the way his body reacted whenever she walked into a room. He stood and fastened his suit jacket. He needed to taste those ruby-red lips of hers; her bewitching smile tugged on his heartstrings like a master puppeteer.

Nash had taken a step, but stopped and turned back to let Tania know that he'd return shortly. Three steps into his short journey to Iris, and the one person he didn't want to see blocked his path.

"Going somewhere?"

His gaze traveled down the length of Eve in her white off-the-shoulder gown. The long, flowing material fell smoothly over her thin body, but Nash could honestly say she no longer had that loin-stirring effect on him.

"Eve," he greeted her drily. "As a matter of fact I *was* going somewhere. Excuse me," he said, with all intention of walking around her.

"Can I talk to you for a minute?" she asked, her hand gripping his arm.

He discreetly pulled out of her grasp. Would he ever

be rid of her? Her constant calls and frequent appearances, with the paparazzi not far behind, made him uncomfortable. He didn't know what she was up to, but Nash didn't trust her state of mind.

"Everything okay here, boss?" Ace asked from behind him. Nash hadn't heard him approach. He, along with several other employees of Platinum Pieces and Dupree Enterprises, were sharing his table.

"Yeah, I was just saying goodbye to Eve." Nash stepped around Eve. He would definitely have to keep an eye on her.

Iris's breath caught in her throat when Nash started toward her, his smooth stride masculine, confident and sexy. Every man in attendance was dressed in black-tie attire, but none worked a tuxedo the way her man did. Black with satin lapels, the jacket draped over his broad shoulders and wide chest like a second skin, cut perfectly for his muscular body. He turned slightly to say something to Tania, and Iris noticed the satin stripe along the outside seam of his long pant leg, complemented by his shiny black wing tips. *Good Lord, as dashing as he looks tonight, he could easily play the role of the next James Bond.*

A little taken aback when a woman in white stepped in front of him, Iris stood rooted in place, curious to see how Nash would respond. She didn't miss the once-over he gave the woman's attire, but was pleased that he didn't seem interested. Iris couldn't tell who the woman was from her vantage point, but the lethal glare Nash gave the stranger when she put her hand on his arm could have cut like a knife. Seconds later, he adjusted his suit jacket and continued toward Iris.

"Come with me." The seductive rumble in his voice demanded her attention. He grabbed her hand and pulled her along, practically knocking her off-balance.

"Nash," she protested and lifted the train of her gown, barely able to keep up with his long strides. "What is wrong with you?" she said in a frustrated whisper.

He said nothing. Instead, he kept walking. He forged his way through small groups of the fund-raiser's attendees huddled in the wide hallway, barely giving a cursory glance at those who greeted him. He glimpsed around corners and peeked inside rooms as if searching for something.

"Nash?" He was going too far and the stilettos on her feet were not meant for jogging through the halls of a hotel. "If you don't tell me what's going on right now, so help me."

Instead of responding, he pulled her into a small meeting room and pressed her body against the nearest wall.

"I've missed you."

His mouth covered hers before she could respond and a zap of desire forced her arms up and around his neck. She would never tire of feeling his soft lips against hers and the way his nearness always sent her pulse racing. She pressed against him, savoring the feel of his hard muscles against her soft curves and loving the touch of his hand roaming over her body. His skillful tongue teased and explored her mouth, stoking the sensual flame growing inside her.

He seemed to be in no hurry to end the kiss, but Iris had a sudden flashback of what took place in the community center's gym weeks ago. She reluctantly pulled back.

"Wow, I'm glad to see you, too," she said, catching her breath.

"Let's get out of here." He continued to run his hands along the curve of her hips until she stepped out of his reach.

"I agree. We really should get back in there." She ran a hand down her dress to smooth it out. "Tania's probably wondering where we disappeared to and since I'm already late, I don't want to miss any more of the program."

"No, I mean let's go home. Your place or mine, I don't care as long as I can bury myself inside you."

Iris's eyes grew large. "What? I thought you meant that we should get out of here and go back to the ballroom. We can't just leave! This is for charity. Besides, do you know how long it took me to get into this dress and get my hair to cooperate?"

He chuckled and kissed her lips. "Nope, but I can't wait to get you out of that dress, and I'm looking forward to messing up your hair. Baby, I want you so bad. I'm tempted to throw you over my shoulder and find an empty room with a bed."

Now it was Iris's turn to laugh. They definitely shared a strong sexual hunger for each other, but she had never seen him so out of control. It was not as if they hadn't made love recently. As a matter of fact, she would never view her kitchen counter the same way again.

She tucked her small beaded purse under her arm and placed her hands on each side of Nash's face. "I love that you want to whisk me away and make mad, passionate love to me, but you're the one who wanted us to finally make an appearance as a couple, despite my misgivings. Are you sure you want to miss this opportunity just because you can't wait for us to do a little somethin'-somethin'?"

He pushed her back against the wall and her purse fell to the floor. Iris's eyes drifted shut and a moan slipped through her lips when he covered her left breast with his large hand, his other hand gripping her butt as he started a slow grind against her. He squeezed and kneaded her breast with the expertise of a man who knew how to please a woman.

"Nash," she said against his lips, knowing it didn't take much for her to climax when his hands caressed any part of her body. She knew they should stop, but she didn't have the strength to push him away.

He captured her lower lip between his teeth, and she groaned into his mouth, desire shooting to her toes.

"Excuse me," someone said from behind Nash, "you guys can't be in here."

Iris stiffened and ducked her head. It was as if someone had dumped a cold bucket of water over her.

Nash cursed under his breath and adjusted his pants, but didn't move from in front of her. It was like déjà vu with the community-center gym and heat rose to Iris's cheeks when she thought about how it must look, them hunched up together against the wall in evening attire, behaving like horny teenagers.

"Sorry," Nash said over his shoulder. "We'll be out of here in a second."

When the intruder left, Nash turned to Iris and they burst out laughing.

"I can't take you anywhere without getting busted,"

Nash joked. They pulled themselves together and sneaked out of the room.

An hour later, they were finishing dessert and the awards portion of the program was about to begin. Iris turned to Nash when she thought she heard his cell phone vibrate. When it vibrated again, he pulled it from his pocket and glanced at the screen. Blood drained from his face.

"What is it?" she said close to his ear.

He handed her the phone for her to read the text while he silently signaled for Ace's attention.

Her eyes grew large when she read: 911, club on fire- Midtown.

"Oh, my God," she whispered.

Nash leaned in close when she handed him his phone back. "I gotta go, but there will be a car outside to take you and Tania home." He placed a quick kiss near her ear. "Love you and I'll be by later," he said and rushed off, Ace matching his long strides.

Love you. Iris's pulse thumped wildly and her hand flew to her chest at Nash's parting words. She tried to slow her erratic breathing, but the more she thought about what he said, the harder her heart pounded. Did he mean it? Did he even realize what he said?

"Iris, are you okay?" Tania asked and grabbed her arm, concern in her eyes. "You don't look so good. What did Uncle Nash say? Is he okay? Did something happen?"

"Oh, sweetheart." She covered Tania's hand with hers. "He's fine. I'm fine," she said, hoping her words sounded calmer than she felt. "Something happened at the club and he needs to go check it out. That's all."

But that wasn't all…not by a long shot.

Chapter 14

Nash knew the moment the words left his mouth that he had messed up. *Love you.* He hadn't said those words to any woman since Audrey, and had no intention of saying them anytime soon.

What was I thinking?

He cursed under his breath and stared out the car window as Ace drove toward Midtown. *Maybe she didn't hear me.* He could only hope. He cared deeply for Iris, but love…

He shook his head and closed his eyes, trying to free his mind from thinking about it any longer. He couldn't worry about that now. He needed to prepare himself for whatever they would find once they arrived at the club

Hours later, after talking with the police and the fire marshal, Nash faced a section toward the back of the club that had sustained the most damage. Shock and anger battled within his gut as he clenched and unclenched his fists. When he opened the club years ago, his intention was to create an environment for others who loved good jazz as much as he did. Now, years of hard work had been destroyed.

He took a staggering walk back to the front of the establishment. Still trying to wrap his brain around the fact that his club had been ruined. The fire marshal told him the cause had been arson, but finding the person or individuals responsible might be impossible.

This is unbelievable, he thought as he continued to take it all in. The soot-covered walls, the water damage, his once beautiful hardwood floors, all of it would need replacing. It would be months before they could reopen.

Tension wrapped around him like a straitjacket, tightening by the minute. Someone had intentionally destroyed what he had worked tirelessly to build.

He cursed through gritted teeth. Anger singed the corners of his control, his insides a bubbling mass of rage. He turned abruptly and unable to stop himself, slammed his fist through a wall, connecting with plaster and a two-by-four.

"Dammit!" he yelled and doubled over holding his hand, wincing when a burning sensation shot up his arm. He stumbled into the wall and dropped to his knees, pain slicing through his hand and wrist.

Ace raced into the room. "What's going on?" He rushed over and helped Nash onto a nearby chair, noticing the bruised knuckles on his dangling hand. "What the hell happened?"

Nash swallowed hard and rocked back and forth, barely able to handle the stinging in his hand. "I stupidly rammed my fist into the wall," he choked out. "I think I might've broken my hand."

"We need to get you to the hospital." Ace grabbed Nash's discarded suit jacket and the keys from the top of the bar, along with Nash's cell phone. "Can you walk?"

Nash nodded, barely withstanding the pain that had now moved to his shoulder.

"We secured the back of the building the best way we could and everything else is locked up."

"Has everyone left?" Nash asked in a voice just above a whisper.

"Yeah, it's just us. Let me hit the lights and then we can go."

Nash's cell phone rang and he knew it was either Iris or Nigel.

"Do you want to answer it?" Ace turned the phone's screen to Nash. *Iris.* "Not right now," he struggled to say. "Just turn it off. I'll call later."

Now he was slow to return her calls because of what he'd said before leaving the fund-raiser. *Love you.* It had slipped out and he wasn't ready to deal with what it really meant.

Iris trudged through the crowded mall, seeing everything, but not really registering anything. The last place she wanted to be was around people. Nash hadn't made it to her place the night of the fund-raiser. It didn't help that he'd only called once in the past forty-eight hours and even then she hadn't talked with him. He'd left a voicemail claiming he was busy. Iris couldn't shake the sense of foreboding that had gripped her the moment she opened her eyes this morning. He called every day. No matter the time, she could always count on his voice being the last voice she heard before she went to sleep each night.

Something is wrong, and I'd bet my law degree that it had nothing to do with the fire. The nagging thought darted around in her head as she followed behind Tania, going from store to store in search the perfect pair of black pants for a dance she was attending at school the following weekend.

"Tania, this is the hundredth store we've been in. It doesn't look like we're going to find the *perfect pair* of black pants. Maybe we should check online, because I've had enough of the mall."

"Okay, but just one more store," Tania insisted, shifting all of her shopping bags to one hand in order to pick up a small satin handbag. She turned it over in her hand several times before checking the price, and then she placed it down and picked up another one.

"Tania," Iris said in a frustrated tone.

Tania sighed and huffed dramatically, but Iris was immune to her theatrics. She had seen it plenty of times. After a couple of months of living together, she learned really quickly that Tania would try any tactic to get her way.

"Are you in a crappy mood because of Uncle Nash?"

"I'm just worried about him." She slung her arm around Tania's shoulder as they headed for the exit.

"Yeah, me, too. He didn't call this morning like he usually does. When I talked with Ms. D., she said he must have gotten in real late because he wasn't home when she went to bed and he had already left the house by the time she woke up." Tania wrapped her arm around Iris's waist. "Every time I call him, I get his voice mail. Do you think he's okay?"

"I'm sure he is, honey."

Iris was tempted to hunt him down. No matter what he was going through with the club, it was no excuse to ignore their telephone calls.

"Why don't we stop by Whole Foods on the way home and pick up dinner? We can veg out in front of the TV, then—"

"Well, isn't this cute."

Oh, great. Eve Vanlough.

"Hi, Tania," Eve greeted. "This is Nash's niece," Eve said to her friend standing next to her. "And…who are you, the nanny?" Both women smirked at Iris.

Tania's shoulders stiffened and Iris wanted to wipe the smug look off Eve's and her friend's faces. She had realized late last night that Eve was the woman in the white gown Nash had been talking to at the fund-raiser.

"No, actually I'm Nash's girlfriend. Excuse us, we were just leaving." Iris intended to guide Tania around the two immaculately dressed women, but Eve stepped in front of them.

"But I'm not done talking with you."

Iris clenched her mouth shut to hold back the angry retort hanging on the edge of her tongue. What in the world had Nash seen in her? Even though she had a cute face and a petite body, Eve still lacked tact and good common sense.

"You must not know who I am."

"She knows who you are, she just doesn't care," Tania retorted. Iris squeezed her shoulder, hoping to keep her quiet.

"Well, you need to understand something, if I catch you dancing with my man again, I will—"

"Excuse me?" Iris said and dropped her arm from around Tania's shoulder, stepping forward. "Are you threatening me? Because apparently you don't know who *I* am. I will have assault charges, harassment charges and anything else I can think of brought against you so fast it will make your head spin."

"Yeah! She's the best defense attorney in town and she doesn't play like that!" Tania added, but closed her mouth when Iris narrowed her eyes at her.

"Oh, please, you don't scare me," Eve said with one hand on her hip and her other waving in the air. "I don't care if you're Judge Mathis. I'm not about to let anyone come between me and my man. Nash and I have been dating for months, so you need to stay the hell away from him."

"You and my uncle aren't dating! He doesn't even like you," Tania snapped and dropped her bags, charging toward the woman. "He dumped you a long time ago. So you need to get a clue!"

"That's enough, Tania," Iris said and pulled her back.

"Oh, Tania, I see you still haven't learned how to stay out of grown folks' business. But if you must know, your uncle and I have been together for months," she said, her eyes trained on Iris.

"Come on, Evie." Her friend grabbed hold of her arm. "Let's go, people are starting to stare."

"Why don't you ask him where he was all night?" She smirked and turned to walk away, but stopped. She looked Iris up and down before saying, "I can't believe you actually thought you had a chance with him."

* * *

Nash stared down at the blueprints spread across the bar, wondering what else would go wrong. Since the fire at his midtown location, he was more determined than ever to get the new club opened. They were ahead of schedule with the renovations, but thanks to a city inspector, some electrical wires would have to be rerouted, which could interfere with the drywallers' schedule.

"Jay, will we have to move the wires for the mounted light fixtures along this wall?" Nash pointed with his left hand to an area on the blueprint where the VIP section would be. He still wasn't used to his right hand being in a splint due to three fractured knuckles, but he had too many things to get done to let it slow him down.

"No. Those are fine," the contractor said.

"What does that mean as far as time and money?" Nash asked.

"Maybe a few hundred dollars. It's not that big of a project since the drywallers haven't put up these walls," Jay said, pointing to the wall that divided the small banquet room and the long closet of the staff's lounge. "Now, it's another story when we tackle the plumbing issue I told you about Monday. We're talking a few thousand dollars and at least twenty man hours to get that done by next Friday."

Nash ran a hand over his head and cursed under his breath. Just once he'd like to get a construction project done on budget and without a lot of setbacks. He let out a weary sigh. Making decisions on two hours of sleep probably wasn't helping, but he trusted Jay. He had overseen the renovations of the midtown club and hadn't steered him wrong.

"All right, do what you have to do to get it done, because as soon as I get the go-ahead from the insurance company, I want to get a crew started on the midtown club as soon as possible."

"No problem. We've got you covered." Jay rolled up the blueprint, stuck it under his arm and grabbed his yellow hard hat from the table. "Don't worry too much. The guys we have are the best and I know they will knock out these issues so we'll hopefully stay ahead of schedule. I'll keep you posted."

"Nash," Nigel called from the back of the building. He stepped into view, standing just outside the staff lounge. "You need to take this," he said, holding up a cell phone.

Seeing the phone reminded Nash that he needed to grab his from the car. He had plugged it in to charge it on the ride into town and had totally forgotten about it.

"It's Tania. She couldn't reach you on your phone, so she called me." Nigel handed him the cell.

"Hey, sweetheart, what's up?" Nash headed toward the back door to the parking lot, where he had parked his car.

"Uncle Nash," Tania sobbed. "Something's wrong with Iris."

Nash slowed his pace as a wave of fear knotted inside him. "Something like what? Is she sick…hurt? Tania, what's happened?"

"I hate Eve, Uncle Nash. I hate her so much. Now Iris might leave us and it'll be all Eve's fault."

"Eve? What does she have to do with anything?" Nash stopped in the middle of the hall, afraid to hear anything that involved Eve. "Tania, I need you to calm down and tell me what happened."

"Iris won't talk to me," she cried. "She's been in her room since we got home and I think she's crying. She was real upset when we got home, but I thought she would feel better by now. She still hasn't come out of her room."

"Tania."

"I tried calling you, but when you didn't answer, I called Aunt Macy, but she's in North Carolina. When she told me to put Iris on the phone…Iris wouldn't talk to her."

"Tania, honey, what happened? What is she upset about?"

Tania relayed the conversation that took place at the mall and Nash thought he would be sick. He leaned against the wall, anger brewing inside his gut as he clenched the cell phone tighter. Iris was the sweetest person he knew and the thought of anyone mistreating her, especially Eve, made him see red.

"Uncle Nash, you have to do something."

"I know, sweetheart. I'm on my way."

"Dammit!" Nash yelled when he disconnected the call, wincing when he bumped his injured hand against the wall. When he realized he didn't have his car keys, he headed back toward the lounge. The past forty-eight hours had been one nightmare after another. He could only imagine what Iris was thinking right now and it didn't help that he hadn't returned any of her calls.

"Is Tania okay?" Nigel asked when Nash stepped across the threshold. Nash handed him his phone back.

"Yeah. No. Oh, hell, I don't know," he said, leaning on the back of a chair. "She's upset because Iris is upset. They had a run-in with Eve and words were exchanged."

Nigel shrugged. "So talk to Iris. All women want is for you to be straight with them. You and Eve haven't been together in months. I'm sure Iris will believe you if you tell her."

Nash rubbed his tired eyes. After being missing in action for the past forty-eight hours, he wasn't sure what Iris would believe. When he didn't say anything, Nigel glared at him.

"You screwed up, didn't you?" Nigel folded his arms across his chest. "Man, what did you do?"

Nash paced to the long table. He grabbed his keys and sunglasses from the top drawer, not in the mood for an "I told you so."

"Okay, don't tell me what's going on, but I thought we agreed that you wouldn't go anywhere without Ace." He pointed at Nash's keys. "Your ex is crazy and I wouldn't put anything past her. If you're not going to let the police know that she's practically stalking you, then you need Ace to follow you around like your shadow."

Nash released a noisy sigh and collapsed into his office chair. "You're right, call him." *This time, Eve has gone too far.*

Chapter 15

Iris lifted her heavy eyelids and glanced around her bedroom. The sun had set and the moon shined through her picture window, casting a stream of light about the room. She must have dozed off. She definitely hadn't meant to stay holed up in her room, but the humiliation lodged in her heart wouldn't allow her to go beyond the double doors of her bedroom.

Why did she think that she could actually have a relationship with Nash that went beyond sex? Eve had been right about one thing. Nash was definitely out of her league and she should have known better than to trust him with her heart.

She had a feeling Eve was baiting her by alluding to the idea that she and Nash had spent the evening together, but Iris couldn't shake her parting words: *Ask him where he was all night.*

"Iris!"

She startled when Nash's voice boomed on the other side of her bedroom door.

"Open the door. We need to talk."

She wasn't ready to see him, wasn't ready to hear his excuses about why he hadn't called or his explanations about where he'd been for the past two days. *And poor Tania.* Iris groaned and held her head. God only knew what she was thinking. Iris couldn't even remember getting them home. The shock of Eve's words had slammed against her like a two-by-four upside her head, leaving her hurt and disoriented.

"Iris." Nash pounded harder.

Maybe if she ignored him, he would go away, leave her to wallow in her own self-pity. She didn't know what bothered her the most, Eve's condescending attitude and hurtful words or the fact that Iris didn't stand up for herself and fight for the man she had fallen deeply in love with.

"Sweetheart, at least let me know that you're okay. Tania is pretty shaken up… We're worried about you."

Iris sighed in resignation, thinking about how her behavior had probably affected Tania. "I'm fine. I just need to be alone."

By the resulting silence, Iris thought he had walked away from the door until he said, "Eve lied about everything. As I told you before, she and I are not together and haven't been for months."

Tears burned the back of Iris's eyes. Why did they have to have this conversation? She should have automatically known that Eve lied, but with Eve and Nash's history and all that Iris had read in the paper about him over the years, there was doubt. In her heart, she believed him, but it still didn't ease the hurt and humiliation she felt. Not knowing where he was last night bothered her more than anything else. He was her man and she had no clue as to where he'd been for the past twenty-four hours.

"Iris…we really need to talk."

He was right. They did. She unlocked the door and let him open it while she trudged to the window, her legs as heavy as her heart. Staring out into the night, her gaze zoned in on nothing in particular, but took in the nighttime view of Buckhead. Lights from neighboring buildings bounced off each other in the darkness and the never-ending traffic below was bumper to bumper, as usual.

She knew the moment Nash came to stand behind her, his fresh scent assailing her nostrils. Yes, they needed to talk, but she still wasn't ready. He had ignored her calls, making her feel as if she didn't matter to him. As if what they had shared over the past couple of months meant nothing. She stiffened when his arm circled the left side of her waist, his hand resting on her stomach. He pulled her against his strong body and she should have resisted, but she couldn't. She wanted—no, she *needed*—to be held, to feel his touch against her body.

Despite her best efforts, tears sprung to her eyes and before she knew it, deep sobs overpowered her and shook her to the core. Nash said nothing. Instead, he held her tighter, placing a kiss in her mounds of curls and let her cry. Iris didn't know how long they stood there, but by the time she had finished shedding her last tear, exhaustion wrapped around her like a two-ton coat. A part of her wanted to stay in the safety of his arms, but remembering why she was holed up in her bedroom in the first place suddenly came to mind. She pried Nash's arm from around her and climbed back into bed. With her knees drawn to her chest and her arms wrapped around her legs, she leaned back against the headboard.

Nash stood watching her from across the room, trying to decide what to say to make her feel better. He gathered his courage and moved to the bed. She had already built a wall between them, but it was up to him to at least knock some of the plaster away. He didn't want her thinking she wasn't good enough for him or that she wasn't desirable. Both of which were far from the truth.

He turned on the lamp next to the bed and stared down at her when it emitted a soft glow around her. A sharp pain pierced his heart seeing the trail of tears flow down her cheeks. He never wanted to be the cause of tears on her lovely face unless they were tears of joy. She was the sweetest woman he had ever met and if anyone wasn't good enough for someone, it was he who wasn't up to par for her.

He had messed up big-time. With other women, when he disappeared or broke things off, it hadn't bothered him. It was the natural course of their relationship. This was different. Iris was different. Hearing her sobs and feeling her body tremble against him, he felt her pain. She was a part of him, occupying a major spot in his heart. He knew before they had gotten seriously involved that she harbored insecurities and compared herself to women he'd been seen with over the years. He thought she was the most beautiful woman he'd ever dated, but after Tania's recap of the afternoon's events, he was pretty sure she had emotionally crawled back into that dark world. Eve's hateful words alone were enough to make any woman have doubt.

"I am so sorry," he said and sat on the bed next to her. "Tania told me what happened and I need you to know that Eve and I are not together. We haven't been since way before you and me."

She glanced at his hand, and then met his gaze. He could see the worry lines deepen across her forehead, but she said nothing.

"It looks worse than it is," he said in answer to her questioning gaze on his bandaged hand. "After dealing with the fire and recovering from the initial shock of seeing my business destroyed, I rammed my fist into a wall. Fractured a couple of knuckles." He lifted his hand slightly.

"Why didn't you tell me?" Her voice wavered and she swallowed before continuing. "I didn't know you were physically hurt. Why did you shut me out?"

Nash turned slightly away from her and sighed. Hunched over, he rested his elbows on his knees, not able to come up with a good response. His reasons for not calling suddenly seemed futile in the big scheme of things. While trying to avoid a conversation about those two words that had slipped through his lips, he unintentionally pushed her away.

"What type of relationship do we have that you can get injured and not tell me? You dealt with the destruction of your jazz club alone instead of allowing me to comfort you, to help in some way. How do you think that makes me feel?"

Nash shook his head. "I don't know." He stared

down at his bandaged hand, then turned to her. "Outside of Nigel, I'm not used to sharing business stuff with anyone." And the only comfort he'd ever received from a woman was in the form of sex, and that was not what he needed that night. But knowing Iris, that wasn't the type of consolation she was referring to. Most times, he felt content just being in her arms and talking about everything, or sometimes about nothing. How could he have let fear of his changing feelings for her keep him away?

"Why are you here?"

Nash furrowed his brows and he looked at her. "How can you even ask me that? I'm here because I care about you and I was worried."

"Oh, so that's where I went wrong the other night." She threw up her hands as if finally understanding. "Since I was so worried about you that night of the fire, instead of me calling and expecting you to call me back, I should have just come and found you."

Nash remained silent. What could he say? She was right. When you cared about someone or were concerned about their well-being, you sought them out. You made sure they were okay. Instead of returning her calls to ease her worry, he disappeared.

"Eve said some awful things to me earlier, but do you know what hurt me the most?"

He shook his head.

"I had no idea where you were that night or where you've been since then. I hadn't heard from *my man* to know whether he was dead or alive or to know whether he was actually *with her* the night of the fire. When she told me to ask where you were that night, my heart sank because I shouldn't have had to ask. I should have known."

Nash turned completely to face her and reached for her hand, kissing the back of it. "Sweetheart, I'm sorry. I screwed up. I don't have a good excuse for not calling you, but I can assure you that I wasn't with Eve or any other woman. I dealt with the fire issue, hung out at the hospital for a few hours and then went home. Yesterday and this morning I had early morning meetings and then this afternoon I met with the contractor of the new club, which is when Tania caught up with me. You have to know that I never meant to hurt you or place doubt in your mind about my feelings for you."

A long silence settled between them and Nash had no idea what she was thinking. He didn't know what else to say. Yeah, he had screwed up, but he didn't want her thinking that he didn't care for her, that he would risk what they had to be with someone else.

"Iris, you have to believe me. I care too much about you to lie to you."

She nodded slightly. "I know…and I believe you." She slipped her hand from his. "But I think we need to take a step back and spend some time apart."

"Why?"

"You have some things you need to work out," she said simply.

He knew exactly what she was referring to. She knew that those two words he spoke the night of the fund-raiser had freaked him out, but instead of calling him out on it, she was letting him off the hook.

"I think you should leave," she said without looking at him.

"But…"

I love you was on the tip of his tongue, but he held them in check. Those were the words that had started this mess in the first place. He wasn't ready for them then, and he sure as hell wasn't ready to deal with them now.

He stood next to the bed. He wanted to tell her how he really felt, but his mouth wouldn't form the words. She was giving him an out. While he should have felt relieved, it felt as if his heart had been ripped out of his chest. She was the best thing that had ever happened to him, and he was about to walk away and risk losing her forever.

Chapter 16

Nash studied the sketches that were spread across the long mahogany conference table, taking in all that the clothing designer explained.

"I thought we would try the peak lapels for this suit jacket instead of the notched ones in order to give the suit a crisper, sharper appearance," the designer said. "Now if you prefer the notch lapel, we can easily make the change..."

For the past hour, Nash found himself tuning in and out of the meeting. He appreciated the details that went into the drawings, but instead of deciding which lapels he preferred or what additional pieces he wanted to add to his new clothing line, he was thinking about Iris. He had hoped the trip to Los Angeles would give him some clarity about his feelings for her, but instead, he was more frustrated than ever. He'd been there for the past week and the only thing that was clear was that he couldn't stand being away from her. And based on his daily conversations with Tania, Iris wasn't managing any better.

"Give us a second, will you?" Nash heard Nigel say to the designer. "Better yet, let's break for lunch and meet back up in a couple of hours."

Nash stood and stepped out onto the balcony of his apartment overlooking the Pacific Ocean, one of many things he missed about leaving L.A. In landlocked Atlanta, he no longer had the luxury of taking off in the middle of the day and walking along the beach, which was where he did his best thinking. He closed his eyes, appreciating the light breeze that kissed the side of his face and the familiar sound of waves crashing against the rocks, which transported him back to calmer times.

"So you want to tell me what's going on with you?" Nigel said when he stepped out onto the private balcony and handed Nash a beer. Nigel had arrived a few days earlier to help finalize the acquisition of a small technology company that they'd been working on for the past year. Nash had known it would only be a matter of time before his longtime friend called him out on his funky attitude.

"You have been acting weird for the past few days and I have tried to give you your space to work out whatever is going on, but enough already. Either tell me what the hell is going on or, so help me, I'm going to beat it out of you."

Nash smirked at his friend, remembering all the times they had joined forces to fight each other's battles while growing up in Compton. But they had never fought each other, at least not physically. His best friend had been there through the good and bad times of his life and he didn't know what he'd do without him.

"It's Iris," he said and took a swig of the cold liquid, feeling himself mellow after the first swallow. "We're taking some time apart."

Nigel leaned against the railing and ran a hand over his mouth and down his goatee. He drank from his beer bottle, then wiped his mouth with the back of his hand. "Taking some time apart, huh? I assume those are her words and not yours."

Nash narrowed his eyes. "What difference does it make whose words they were?"

"Oh, there's a difference, all right. Normally you're the one who's putting up the walls or requesting time apart, or breaking things off. For as long as I can remember, you've never been on the receiving end of 'taking some time apart' and I, for one, am shocked by how you're handling it."

Nash wanted to wipe the smug look off his friend's face. He didn't have to ask what Nigel meant. He knew. Nash had never lacked the company of a female; if anything there were times when he longed to *not* be the object of one's desire.

"I've seen what you're like after moving on from a woman. How many times did you break up with a woman and before the day was over you were going out with someone else? Or what about those times when you showed up at the club and drinks were on the house for all the men?"

"That happened one time." That was after he broke up with Eve or, at least, after the first time he told Eve they were done. He was so glad to be rid of her that buying drinks for all the guys at the club that night seemed to be the right thing to do. He had no doubt that most of them had either had an Eve in their life or were still recovering from having a woman like her.

"You normally celebrate when you find yourself *free* again. So why is this different? Why are you acting like you just lost your best friend?"

Nash studied his friend for a moment, knowing that Nigel knew good and well the answer to his own questions. Spending time with Iris had become Nash's favorite pastime. Her intelligence, humor and selfless heart were everything he didn't realize he wanted in a woman. He thought about their active sex life. She was as passionate in the bedroom as she was in the courtroom. He shook his head at the thought and stepped back into the apartment. Nigel followed behind him.

Nash placed his empty bottle on the granite countertop and strolled to the living room, which was decorated in silver and black. He dropped down on the long leather sofa and propped his feet up on the marble end table. The past few days had been hell. He didn't know when it happened, but he knew he had fallen madly and passionately in love with Iris. At first, he had just wanted to get to know her better while he got through his legal issues, but then the sexual attraction between them couldn't be ignored. Now he found himself wanting to spend every waking hour with her.

"You might as well admit that you're in love with her," Nigel said from the pristine kitchen that overlooked the living room. From the built-in refrigerator, he pulled out the makings of a sandwich. Whenever Nash knew he would be in town, he'd have the housekeeper stock the refrigerator. "Don't worry. It happens to the best of us."

Years ago, Nash had promised himself that he would never allow another woman access to his heart, but somehow Iris had penetrated the wall he had built around it. Even traveling across the country didn't decrease his need to be near her. If anything, it made it worse.

"Let me give you a piece of advice," Nigel continued, as if Nash's lack of response meant he should keep talking. "When you find *the one,* you do whatever you have to do to hold on to her. If you've screwed up, you swallow your pride and say, 'I'm sorry' and that you can't live without her. Whatever it takes to get her back."

When silence filled the space, Nash glanced at Nigel, who was piling turkey, ham, tomatoes, cheese, lettuce and pickles onto a long thin loaf of French bread, reminding Nash that he hadn't eaten all day.

"I've seen the way you look at Iris and how you are with her." Nigel cut his sandwich and didn't look up. "I'll be the first to admit I thought it was a bad idea when you first showed an interest in her. We both know your track record with women, but you've changed," he said and finally cast his gaze at Nash. "She changed you."

Nash placed his feet on the floor and sighed. He hated to admit it, but Nigel was right. Nash had to do whatever it took to get Iris back. There was no way he was going to live the rest of his life without her.

He stood and walked across the room, his gaze zoned in on the long sandwich stuffed with meat and vegetables. It reminded him of their childhood, when they'd go to one of their houses after school and build a mile-high sandwich with whatever they could find in the refrigerator.

Nash grabbed a plate from the cabinet near the sink, his mouth watering at how good he knew the sandwich would taste. "Can I get part of that?"

"Hell, no. Make your own."

Iris stared off into space.

It was late Friday evening and she was still at work when most everyone else had left for the day. She propped her elbows on her desk and rubbed her tired eyes, disappointed that she didn't have anything to look forward to this weekend except for work. Even Tania had plans to spend the next couple of days with Macy and her goddaughter. Candace and Tania were the same age and, despite only knowing each other for a couple of months, got along like sisters.

"All right, Iris, I'm heading out," Melissa said, walking over to Iris's desk carrying a FedEx package. "This came while you were on the conference call."

"Oh, good, thanks. I was worried I wouldn't get it today." Iris began opening the large envelope.

"Is there anything else you need before I leave?"

Iris pulled a folder and several stapled documents from the envelope. "Nope, but thanks. Go on home and enjoy your weekend. I appreciate your staying this late."

"No problem." Melissa headed toward the door, then stopped and turned. "Oh, before I forget, Noelle said that she hopes to have some good news for you soon. She stopped by on her way out, but you were still on your call."

"Oh, okay, thanks."

Iris knew it was probably regarding Tania's hearing in less than two weeks. The date seemed to come up quick, and the thought of their living situation changing was bittersweet. She was happy Tania and Nash had fulfilled the court's requirements, and that it looked as though Nash would get Tania back soon. On the other hand, she didn't know what she would do without Tania in the house. It was bad enough that she and Nash were no longer together, but not seeing Tania either was almost too much to think about.

Iris shook off the sudden melancholy and stood. She wouldn't think about that day until she had to. With several files in her hand, she walked across her office, her bare feet sinking into the plush carpet. She had slipped off her shoes over an hour ago, unable to stand the four-inch heels any longer.

"Are you planning to work all weekend?"

Iris startled at the deep, velvety voice. Her racing heart beat double time, knowing who she would find standing behind her. She turned slowly from the file cabinet to find Nash's large frame leaning against the doorjamb. Tall, immaculately dressed and looking sexier than any man had a right to, he locked his penetrating gaze on her.

She held his gaze. "No, not all weekend, but maybe a big chunk of it." She wondered if her voice sounded as shaky as she felt. It seemed as if she hadn't seen him in months, but it had only been ten days. God, she had missed him. Tears stung the back of her eyes, but there was no way she was going to cry. It was her decision to put some space between them and she had lived with that…until now.

Her gaze lingered on his sexy lips, which had

brought her more pleasure than she had ever experienced in her life. There wasn't a day that had gone by that she hadn't thought about him, wondered where he was or what he was doing. How many times had erotic flashbacks of their lovemaking sprung to mind, making her wish she were in his arms? A few days ago, Noelle had tried setting her up on a blind date, but Iris couldn't imagine herself with another man. If she couldn't have Nash, she would rather live the rest of her life alone.

"I've missed you," he said. He pushed away from the doorframe and closed the door. He moved toward her, his long graceful strides reminding her of a cheetah, easing up on his prey. The intensity in his eyes held her captive. No man had ever looked at her the way he looked at her now, adoration mixed with longing and need, only making her want to jump into his arms and never let go.

She glanced down at his hand, noticing it was still bandaged, but without the splint that he'd had on it when she'd seen him last.

"Before you throw me out, or have me thrown out, there's something I have to say."

She licked her lips nervously. "I would never have you thrown out. I might ask you to leave, but never thrown out."

Nash flashed that sexy grin that always made her body throb for his touch. "Good to know."

Iris swallowed hard and fiddled with the buttons on her silk blouse, suddenly finding the garment excruciatingly warm. Nash standing so close didn't seem real. He had called her the day before he was heading to L.A. and once while he was there, but their conversation had centered on Tania.

"So what did you want to say?" She pushed a wayward curl from her face, discreetly brushing away the perspiration that beaded on her forehead.

"Something I should have said weeks ago." He stepped closer and pulled her into his arms, his hands resting just above her hip bones, his tempting lips only inches from hers. She had missed him so much. There was no way she would pull away. "I love you," he said huskily. "I love you so damn much I physically ache. I can't stand being away from you."

She searched his eyes, hoping to determine that he was telling the truth, that he meant what he was saying. For weeks she had waited, hoping to hear him say those words to her again. Needing to hear them and believe what she had hoped was true. That he loved her as much as she loved him.

Tears sprung to her eyes. "I love you, too, and I have missed you more than I ever thought possible. I'm sorry for everything. I'm sorry for pushing you…"

Her words lodged in her throat when his mouth swooped down and covered hers. No one had ever kissed her with as much passion, with as much love as Nash. He made her feel like she was the most important person in his world. He grabbed her butt and crushed her to him. Aroused by the mere feel of the bulge between his thighs pressing against her pelvis, Iris wrapped her arms around his neck and deepened the kiss. When they had first made love months ago, he unleashed a sexual hunger that she didn't know existed, but that she definitely wanted him to feed.

"Nash," she whimpered against his lips, wanting more, needing more.

"I know, sweetheart."

* * *

With nimble fingers, Nash made quick work of her blouse, unbuttoning it and yanking it off, leaving her in a pink satin-and-lace bra. He hungrily devoured her lips, his tongue tangling with hers as his fingers teased her taut nipples through the thin material of her bra, sending a rush of heat to his groin. He needed her like a thirsty man needed water. How could he have walked away from her, knowing how much he loved her?

He licked, nipped and sucked her tongue until she moaned into his mouth. One taste of her sweet lips and he'd known he wouldn't be able to stop.

She looped an arm around his waist and rubbed her curvy body against his. She had clearly gotten bolder over the past couple of months. He sucked in a breath when her hand made contact with his swollen erection and he ground against her palm, knowing that if he kept it up, their little reunion would be over before it got started.

He pulled back and undid her bra, letting it tumble to the floor, one breast falling into his hands. He stroked and teased her nipple between his thumb and forefinger before his tongue went to work, swirling around the dark peak.

"Nash." She sucked in a breath when he squeezed and caressed her other breast. "Enough!" She grabbed hold of the front of his shirt and her nipple slipped from his mouth. "I don't need foreplay, so stop screwing around."

He grinned when she backed him up against a nearby wall. His pulse picked up when his gaze zoned in on her breasts, turning him on even more. He unfastened her pants while her hands worked feverishly to pull his shirt away from his body. Buttons flew across the room, but he didn't care. All he wanted was what she wanted, to have their bodies come together as one.

They clawed at each other's clothes, removing everything until they were panting and standing in only their birthday suits. Nash bent down and snatched his wallet from his pants pocket, quickly removing a condom and slipping it on.

He spun Iris around, her back against the wall. "I can't wait to get inside you."

He stood between her legs and nudged them farther apart seconds before he lunged upward into her moist opening. *Heaven.* That's what it felt like when her muscles contracted tightly around him. He loved that she was only a couple inches shorter than him, allowing their bodies to line up perfectly in all the right areas.

Her eyes grew round and she chirped in surprise when he lifted her off the floor, his fingers gripping the soft flesh of her derriere. His hand hadn't completely healed, but the sweet taste of her lips and her body grinding against his made the pain worth it. She wrapped her long legs around him and he used the wall to help support her as he plunged upward, in and out, going deeper and deeper, loving the feel of her in his arms.

It had been torture not seeing her, holding her and being inside her. His heart hammered against his rib cage as she squeezed her thighs and he felt himself grow thicker within her.

He cursed under his breath at the intense pleasure. "Iris..." he ground through clenched teeth, knowing his control was slipping as he slid in and out of her.

Her breathing became labored and her eyes were

tightly closed as her nails dug deeper into his shoulder. He knew she was teetering on the edge.

"Sweetheart, look at me." He didn't let up as he continued to move, but he wanted to see those beautiful eyes of hers.

"Nash," she sobbed, her eyes still slammed shut. "I can't hold…"

"Look at…" he said raggedly as his own control began to slip. "I want you looking at me when we come."

"Nash!" Her eyes flew open and she bucked against him wildly. In the moment, he saw that it was almost over for her, so he lowered his mouth over hers, swallowing the yell he knew would erupt.

She came violently, screaming into his mouth, clawing at his back and shoulders, her body overpowered by her intense orgasm. He ripped his mouth from hers and he growled roughly when he started coming, gripping her tightly when his body convulsed with its own powerful release.

"Oh my God, oh my God," Iris chanted as her body continued to shake violently. "Nash!" she whimpered and collapsed against him.

On wobbly legs, he lowered her feet to the floor, his knees so weak that he could no longer hold either of them up. They slid to the plush carpet in a tangled heap.

He chuckled, still trying to catch his breath. "That… was amazing." He found her lips and kissed her slowly.

"What is it with you and always wanting to take me up against a wall?" she asked, breathless, her words coming out in spurts.

"Beds are highly overrated." He nipped her ear with his teeth and started a path of kisses along her neckline. "I'm thinking that maybe we should finish this on your desk."

She moaned and draped her arms around his neck. "Lead the way, my love. Lead the way."

Chapter 17

"Well, someone's in a good mood," Noelle said when she sauntered into Iris's office. "You're humming to yourself, got your hair piled on top of your head all sexily—" Noelle flicked her hand toward Iris "—and you're smiling. As a matter of fact, you've been smiling hard all week. I would ask why, but I have a feeling I already know."

Iris lowered her head to hide the grin that was slowly spreading across her face, as she recalled how she and Nash had christened her office a week ago. In less than three months, she had had more firsts with Nash Dupree than she had in all of her life. There was something about the man that made her want to live for the moment and deal later with any consequences. Which is what she'd done when the cleaning lady had walked in on them last Friday night. Thank goodness they had slipped back into their clothes before Iris heard the keys rattling in the door.

"Well, I have some news that will add to your happiness." Noelle sat in one of the upholstered chairs in front of Iris's desk. "We just found out that the drugs were definitely planted on Tania and we know who did it."

"Who?"

"One of Tania's friends."

"What?"

"Yeah. It sounds like her friend Tiffany—and I use the term 'friend' lightly—stashed the package in Tania's bag before leaving school. Tiffany's brother attends the same school and has been arrested twice for drug possession. A third arrest meant he would serve time."

"But I'm sure Tiffany didn't know they would be pulled over. Why would she plant the package in Tania's bag while at school?"

Noelle shrugged. "Why do teenagers do half the things they do? Tiffany found the weed in her brother's bedroom that morning. Not wanting him to get caught with it, she took it to school."

Iris stood and shook her head, pacing behind her desk. "That's crazy. She could have tossed it instead of putting it in Tania's bag." Iris tried keeping a grip on her anger, but felt it slipping out of her grasp the more she thought about the situation. She had caught Tiffany smoking in her downstairs bathroom one night when Tania had her friends over. "Ugh, this makes me so angry. How can she call herself Tania's friend if she's setting her up like that?"

"Hey, don't get mad at me. I'm just the messenger," Noelle blurted out. "Tania said she and the girl had a disagreement a few weeks ago. Tania called her brother a pothead and all hell broke loose."

"So what made Tiffany come forward?"

"She didn't, her parents did. They said Tiffany had been suffering from nightmares and finally told them everything."

"I'm shocked they would implicate their son, knowing he would have to serve time."

"It sounds like he has a real bad drug problem. They tried rehab, but that didn't work. They felt turning him in was the only way to help him. The mom suspected that he had started back on drugs, but didn't know how bad it was until she found cocaine in his room."

"That's awful," Iris said and leaned against the back of her chair. Tania's court date was scheduled for next Tuesday, and this was just the news they needed to ensure that all went well when they went before the judge. "I'm happy they found the person responsible for planting the drugs, but I hate seeing a family go through something like this."

Noelle stood. "Yeah, me, too. But there is a bright side," she said over her shoulder on her way to the door.

"What's that, besides the obvious?"

"You got a chance to meet Nash Dupree, who turned out to be the man of your dreams."

Iris smiled as Noelle walked out of her office. That was definitely the bright side. She couldn't wait to tell him about the new development. She glanced at her watch. *Four o'clock.* Tonight was the grand opening of the new club and he wanted her by his side throughout the evening. She grabbed her jacket, purse and umbrella from the coat stand in the corner. She needed to head home so that she could make herself beautiful for her man.

Nash walked into his new club and a slow smile spread across his face when he heard the sounds of Bill Evans, one of the greatest jazz pianists, flowing through the house speakers. Nash whistled along with the smooth tunes of the CD, remembering why he loved jazz. He walked through the semidark hall toward the front of the building, admiring the finishing touches he saw along the way. Things had come together nicely.

He made it to the dining area and glanced toward the stairs leading to the second floor where the VIP lounge was located. The electrician had finally fixed the lighting problem on the staircase. Now the lights between the wrought-iron railing slats illuminated a nice bluish color over each stair, providing just enough light to keep anyone from stumbling.

“Are you ready for tonight?” Grant, the club’s manager, asked when he turned the corner and walked into the dining area.

“I think so. Question is, are you ready?” Nash asked and shook his extended hand. Grant had been the assistant manager of Nash’s midtown club until Nash offered him the position of head manager of Platinum Pieces–Buckhead.

“I’m as ready as I’ll ever be.” He laughed and leaned against one of the belly-bar tables, a white tablecloth draped over it. “But seriously, we’re all set. Ace is downstairs talking to the security team and I will be briefing the servers shortly.”

"What about that black sofa in the VIP lounge? Did it get switched out?"

"Yep, the company apologized profusely and said they don't know how the mixup happened. They confirmed that six black leather lounge sofas with the cherrywood legs were ordered. They're thinking that something must have gotten screwy when loading the truck. At any rate, it's been taken care of."

"Good to hear." Nash slapped him on the shoulder before he headed up the stairs to his office. "Oh." He stopped and turned. "Iris should be here in about an hour. Let her know that I'm in my office."

"Will do."

Nash finished climbing the stairs and smiled. Maybe he and Iris could christen this space the way they had hers last week. There was definitely something appealing about making love to her in an office.

He chuckled, pushed open his office door, and froze. "What the hell are you doing in here?" he roared.

Eve stood near the small bar in the corner of the office, sipping a drink.

"Hey, baby, can I fix you a drink?"

The trench coat she wore, despite the seventy-degree weather outside, was tied at her waist. It revealed one long, tanned leg. Nash didn't want to think about what she had on underneath, but knowing her, it wouldn't be much.

"What are you doing here?" he asked again, not bothering to ask how she got in. He was starting to think she was a ghost, able to walk through halls and walls without being detected. That was the only way to explain how she always managed to appear out of nowhere at the oddest times.

He moved across the plush carpet and over to his office chair. Ace had installed an emergency button under the desk and if he couldn't get Eve to leave on her own, he knew Ace would.

"I came by to congratulate you on the new club… and to apologize."

Nash narrowed his eyes. Eve wasn't the apologizing type, always feeling that people should bow down and worship the ground she walked on.

She sipped her drink and sauntered to the front of the desk, twirling the sash that was barely holding her coat closed.

"I know I have been giving you a hard time the past few months, and I'm sorry."

"You're sorry?" he asked, waiting for her to share the real reason for her sudden appearance. After her run-in with Iris, she'd showed up at his house late the same night, refusing to leave. Not only did he have to call the police to remove her from the premises, but the next morning he took out a restraining order against her. A call right now and he could have her arrested.

"Why have you been stalking me?"

"I haven't been stalking you," she said indignantly.

"What in the hell would you call it?"

She sat her glass down and folded her arms across her chest. "I've been trying to get you to understand that we belong together. Nash, can't you see…I love you."

Anger crept up his spine. "So you have stalked me and set my club on fire because you're in love with me?"

She glanced down at the sash in her hand and said nothing. As far as Nash was concerned, her silence proved his hunch—she was behind it all. Up until a few minutes ago, he hadn't been sure.

She glanced up, tears lacing her eyelashes. "Nash, we were once very good together. I can't believe you didn't come to me when all those things happened to you. There was a time when I could make all of your worries go away, make you forget about the troubles of your day."

Nash stared at her, dumbfounded. "That's what this was all about? You set stuff up to happen to me and then I'm supposed to run to you for comfort?" he roared and leaned forward, his palms on the desk. "Have you lost your damn mind?"

A wicked smirk slid onto her lips. "Of course not, silly. But I think you probably forgot how much pleasure I brought you." She undid the sash of her coat and it slid off her shoulders and onto the floor, leaving her with only a white see-through teddy on.

"Get out of my office and stay the hell away from me!"

Nash pushed the emergency button seconds before a quick knock came from the other side of the door and it swung open.

"Nash, I have some good…" Iris said as she stepped into view, but stopped short. She glanced from Nash to Eve and then back at Nash, shock distorting her beautiful face. Her hand flew to her chest, tears welling in her eyes as she backed away. "How could you?" she said in a tone just above a whisper before she bolted out of the room.

Damn.

"Iris!" He hurried from around the desk and to the

door. Ace showed up in that moment, his gun drawn, and blocked his exit.

Nash swung back around to face Eve, anger driving his long strides toward her as fear showed on her face.

"If anything happens to her, or if I can't get her back—" his face was inches from hers as rage churned in his gut "—I will make you regret the day you ever met me."

He snatched his keys from his desk and glared at her before turning to Ace.

"Have her arrested for harassment, ignoring a restraining order and…for arson. I want her ass behind bars."

Iris sped down the street despite torrential rain pounding against her windshield. She couldn't believe Nash would cheat on her. They hadn't been back together a good week and he was already in the arms of another woman, and not just anyone. Iris wished she would have taken the time to scratch the little hussy's eyeballs out before she bolted from the room.

"How could I have been so stupid?" She slammed her hand against the steering wheel, tears clouding her view. She had trusted him and look where it got her! *Stupid, stupid, stupid. How could someone who is supposed to be so smart not see this coming?*

She dodged in and out of traffic and hopped on the highway heading north toward Macy's house. A bolt of lightning lit the sky and Iris jumped at the sudden roar of thunder. She decreased her speed as the rain came down harder, limiting her visibility even more. She swiped at her tears. She just needed to get away, needed time to think.

Iris heard her cell phone ring. It had rung several times since leaving the club and she knew it was Nash. There was no way he could talk his way out of what she had seen with her own eyes. The sight of Eve standing before him in only that lacy getup was enough to make Iris want to throw up. A week ago, that was her standing before him in nearly nothing, prepared to give him anything he wanted.

Her violent emotions matched the intensity of the storm brewing outside, and they gripped her with such force she thought she would die. Never had she loved a man as she had Nash. There was nothing she wouldn't have done for him and this was the thanks she received! *How could he?* How could he throw away what they had after all that they had been through? He'd sworn to her that he and Eve were over, yet she was in his face the moment Iris's back was turned.

An hour later, Iris pulled into Macy's driveway, hoping that her sister had already left for the grand opening. She would've preferred to go home, but Tania was there and Iris didn't want Tania to see her like this again. Thinking of Tania made her cry harder. In a few days, Tania and Nash's legal issues would be over and Tania would be back home with her uncle. This was not how things were supposed to end.

Iris glanced in her rearview mirror and wiped her face, trying to pull herself together. Terrible regrets assailed her, but this wasn't the first time her heart had been broken. She survived before; she would survive again.

She grabbed her purse and bolted out of the car, running to the door as fast as her four-inch heels would take her. Searching for the key on her key ring, she prayed that Macy wouldn't still be there. No sooner had she thought that, Macy swung the door open.

"Where have you been?" she yelled. "I've been worried sick about you ever since Nash called and told me what happened. How could you just take off like that in this weather without giving him a chance to explain what you *thought* you saw?"

"I know what I saw!" Iris stomped past her sister and didn't stop until she reached the kitchen, not caring that she had tracked water into the house.

"As an attorney, you know better than anyone that you don't convict someone until you hear all of the arguments, or whatever the hell terms you people use," Macy shouted, her arms flailing. "You already know that this Eve person is a troublemaker. Why would you take off like that?"

"You didn't see how she was dressed. I know Nash and how he feels about sex in his office."

Iris knew the moment the words left her mouth from the shocked expression on Macy's face that she had said too much.

"Well, don't stop now, Iris," Nash's voice boomed from the doorway of the kitchen. She swung around, nearly tipping over on her heels, shocked to see him. "You didn't tell her that you're the *only* woman that I have ever made love to in any office or that you're the *only* woman that I ever want to do that with."

"Okay, you know what—" Macy covered her ears "—this is way too much information." She rushed out of the kitchen, but yelled, "And don't you dare do anything on my kitchen counter."

* * *

Nash wanted to be mad, but he couldn't. Iris was dressed in the sexiest outfit he'd ever seen her in, and she took his breath away. The steel-gray strapless dress stopped a few inches above her knees and fit every inch of her curvaceous body to perfection. Despite her red, puffy eyes and her hair, originally pinned up on top of her head, but now curling around her shoulders, she was still the most beautiful woman in the world to him.

"You look amazing," he said and moved closer, encouraged that she hadn't moved a muscle since he walked into the room. "What do I have to do to prove to you that you're the only woman in my life, that you're the only one I want?"

She swallowed but didn't speak. Her chest heaved, bringing more attention to her bountiful breasts, and Nash wanted to do just what Macy warned them not to do—take Iris right then and there.

"I can swear on mine and Tania's lives that I will never, ever want another woman the way that I want you, but somehow, I doubt that would be enough for you." He stopped in front of her. Her enticing scent was doing wicked things to his body, sending sparks of desire to his every nerve ending.

She still didn't speak, so he kept going. "Maybe if I drop down on one knee—" which he did "—and ask you to spend the rest of your life with me, so that I can prove every day how much I love you and need you… then maybe you'll believe me."

Keeping his gaze on hers, he pulled a small velvet box from the inside pocket of his tuxedo jacket. Tears streamed down her face, and her hands covered her mouth.

"I had planned to do this at the club tonight, but my uninvited guest ruined my plans, so I guess I have to go to plan B." He opened the black box and held it out. "Iris Marie Sinclair, would you do me the honor of being my wife?"

She cried out and lunged into his arms, practically knocking him over.

"Yes, yes, I would be honored to be your wife." She slung her arms around his neck and crushed her lips to his.

Epilogue

Three months later

"I now pronounce you husband and wife. You may kiss the bride."

Iris handed her wedding bouquet to Macy, her maid of honor, and then stepped into Nash's arms. When his mouth covered hers, she melded her body against his and it was as if the rest of the world disappeared, leaving only the two of them. Every time he kissed her, he roused a passion that started at the top of her head and worked its way to the tip of her toes, making her want even more.

His mouth teased hers, taking her lower lip between his teeth nipping, sucking and licking.

Nash wrapped his arm around Iris's waist and pulled her close to his side. He placed a kiss against her temple. "I love you, sweetheart."

"Oh, Nash. I love you, too." Tears rolled down her cheeks and Macy shoved tissues into her hands. Iris had thought for sure she would get through the wedding without crying, but Nash always found a way to do something sweet and unexpected.

For the next few minutes, Mikale serenaded them, one song after another. If anyone had told Iris a year ago that she would be marrying the man of her dreams on a beautiful island, with the Caribbean Sea as the backdrop, she would have never believed it. She had once thought of her life as a nightmare, losing her mother at a young age, going from foster home to foster home, and then working long hours with no one to go home to. But now she was living a fairy tale.

When the singer finished, he congratulated them and agreed to stay for the reception. Nash pulled her into his arms and kissed her again, promising to make their honeymoon a time to remember.

"Okay, you two, save some for later," Janna said from behind them and everyone laughed. Nash had flown her whole family to Ocho Rios, Jamaica. He had made a special trip to New Jersey to escort his new mother-in-law, who was afraid of flying, to the wedding. Mama Adel and Ms. D. got along beautifully, enjoying being around the "young folks," as they referred to them.

"Everyone, may I have your attention?" the wedding planner said. "Once the couple and wedding party finish taking pictures, the reception will be held on the terrace." She pointed to the area of round tables near the bandstand gazebo.

When the photographer said he wanted a shot with her, Nash and Tania, Iris glanced around wondering where Tania had disappeared to. She finally spotted her, several yards away, staring out into the ocean.

Iris squeezed Nash's hand. "I'm going over there to check on Tania. I'll be right back."

"All right." He pulled her in for a kiss before releasing her hand. "Hurry back."

"Tania, honey, are you okay?" Iris asked when she got closer. She wrapped her arm around Tania's bare shoulders. As one of the bridesmaids, Tania wore a light gray off-the-shoulder dress that stopped just below her knees. "Why are you over here by yourself?"

She glanced up at Iris, tears lacing her eyelashes. "I was thinking how happy I am that you and Uncle Nash got married. Out of all of the women he dated, you're the only one we both liked."

Iris chuckled. "Well, I'm glad to hear that."

She was also glad that Eve was out of their lives, at least for now. They had hoped she would spend years behind bars, but it looked as if she would only pay a hefty fine and spend a few months in jail. Iris couldn't care less what happened to her, as long as she stayed away from her family.

"So you're okay with us living under the same roof permanently?"

Tania smiled. "Definitely. I always wanted to have a mom. I only remember bits and pieces about my mother. What I remember most were her hugs. Kinda like the way you hug me, making me feel safe and loved."

Iris wrapped both her arms around Tania and kissed the top of her head. "I will always love you. Actually, I should be thanking you."

"For what?"

"For bringing us all together. Though I don't want you to ever get into trouble again, I have to admit, something good came out of you getting picked up by the cops."

Tania grinned. "Yeah, I planned it that way."

Iris reared back. "What?" she said, louder than she meant to. "Young lady, if you tell me you intentionally got into trouble, I'm going to wring your neck!"

"I'm kidding, I'm kidding! I didn't plan any of it, promise."

"What's going on over here?" Nash wrapped his arm around Iris's waist and nudged Tania's shoulder like he often did. "Are you causing trouble?" he asked Tania.

"Nope, just trying to get a rise out of Iris." She grinned.

"Well, be gentle with her," Nash said and placed a soft kiss against Iris's cheek. "I don't want you to scare her away before she starts the adoption process."

Tania's mouth dropped open. "Adoption process?"

Now it was Iris's and Nash's turns to grin. "Well, if it's okay with you, I'd like to adopt you," Iris said.

Tania looked from Iris to Nash, and then back at Iris. "Yes!" She jumped up and down, then wrapped her arms around both of them. "Then can I call you 'Mom'?"

Iris hand flew to her chest, trying not to cry. She hadn't thought that far ahead. Since Nash had legally adopted Tania years ago and she still called him Uncle Nash, Iris hadn't expected her to call her "Mom."

"Of course, honey." Iris kissed the top of her head.

"Hold up," Nash chimed in. "Why is it that you want to call Iris 'Mom,' and you call me 'Uncle Nash' and not 'Dad'?"

Tania thought for a moment and then shrugged. "I'm not sure, but now that you mention it, I think 'Dad' has a nice ring to it."

They all laughed and Nash wrapped his arms around his two favorite women, directing them back to their small wedding party.

Iris whimpered in her sleep and snuggled closer.

Nash stared down at her and ran his fingers through her hair. After several rounds of lovemaking, he didn't think he would ever get enough of his wife. He still couldn't believe he was married. Never in a million years would he have thought that he was capable of being someone's husband, but he was, and he planned to be the best. Iris deserved nothing less.

She stirred next to him and slowly opened her eyes, a smile forming on her inviting lips.

"Hi."

"Hi, yourself." He slid the back of his fingers down her cheek. "Have I mentioned lately that you're amazing, Counselor?"

"You might have mentioned it a time or two."

She pushed him back and climbed on top of him. Lately, she had been getting bolder, taking charge in the bedroom, and he had no complaints. From now on, his mission in life was to make sure she was happy and wanted for nothing.

"Have I also mentioned that the women in your life made me promise to be at your beck and call for the duration of our honeymoon?"

She grinned down at him. "No, I don't think you mentioned that."

"Well, I'm here for you. Whatever you need."

She turned serious and stretched out on top of him, her naked body crushed against his. She traced her finger around his lips. “All I want is your love.”

* * * * *